PROTECTING HIS WITCH

KEEPERS OF THE VEIL

PROTECTING HIS WITCH

KEEPERS OF THE VEIL

ZOE FORWARD

Entangled Publishing, LLC
10940 S Parker Rd
Suite 327
Parker, CO 80134
rights@entangledpublishing.com

Amara is an imprint of Entangled Publishing, LLC.

Edited by Allison Collins
Cover design by Miguel Parisi
Cover photography by Honored_member, Pla2na, Deviney Designs, Bokeh Blur Background, and Dn Br/Shutterstock

Manufactured in the United States of America

First Edition October 2014

To Bert, who never compromises for the status quo.

Chapter One

Buzzing electrified Kat Ramsey's brain. She jolted upright in bed, now fully awake. Her body tingled, and her chest cranked so tight that she gasped for air. This signaled an imminent jump to a different reality. Air chilled her upper body. One glance down and…she was naked? *Oh, no. I can't jump to that other place naked!*

The jumps to the Otherworld came at random. And, thank God, they didn't happen often. The last time was five years ago, after a motorboat explosion killed her parents and threw her from the boat.

She never slept bare out of terror that this might happen. *Clothes…get clothes.* Her retinas burned as she squinted against the early light of dawn filtering through the dorm room's mini-blinds. *Where am I?* This wasn't her room.

She rocked to move out of the bed, but found herself anchored. She yanked the sheet off the lower half of her body. A male arm draped her lap. She wheezed out, "Oh God."

The hand curved around her bare thigh. And caressed. The gentle sweeps of his fingers sensitized every nerve in the vicinity. Half of her mind freaked out that there was a guy stroking her nude thigh. The other part recognized the hand, and him. And screamed, *Oh yeah.* The tug-o-war in her brain turboed the humming into pulsating pain.

Memories of the wild things she'd done with him—Matt Ryan—slideshowed in her mind. Maybe the pain in her skull was the aftereffect of those Purple Passion drinks and not an imminent reality-shift warning.

His fingers continued to electrify the skin of her thigh.

"Where am I?" she asked. This room, and *him,* were in that different reality, Otherworld as she liked to call it. Last night, she'd entered *her* dorm room in her world after a study marathon to discover her four-month super crush and chem-lab partner sucking face with her roommate. The next minute she'd reality jumped into a dark corner of a rowdy frat party. With her emotions running high, she'd immediately dipped a sixteen-ounce plastic cup into a barrel of purple drink.

His fingers teased across her lap as he rolled to his back and threw an arm over his face. An intricate blue Celtic tattoo decorated the inside of his right wrist.

Her heart raced. She denied the urge to bolt from the bed, not out of respect for his feelings, but out of self-preservation against the pounding inside her skull.

"My head is killing me." He struggled to a sit-prop against the headboard and pressed his thumb into the side of his forehead. At least he, too, suffered. The guy had consumed as many of those drinks as she. Her gaze drifted down his body. The guy was stunning from buzz cut to chiseled chest. The striped sheet barely covered the substantial bulge in his lap. As her mind filled in the gaps hidden by the sheet, her cheeks burned.

Holy cow, she'd just slept with the hottest guy in the universe. She, the super science geek. The you-go-girl side of her brain wahooed. The rational side of her brain spat out a resounding, *Oh shit.* She'd never slept with a guy before. She definitely didn't do one-nighters. She'd had several major crushes and three awkward dates since she started undergrad a year and a half ago. And she'd gotten drunk at one frat rush party, but even then she'd kept her clothes on. Other guys barely pushed her body beyond lukewarm. She remained in control and her mind rational, which meant she talked herself out of proceeding in every case.

Until Matt. One kiss and she'd practically attacked him when he discovered her in that dark corner of the party last night. He'd been the one to put on the brakes, renew their drinks, and try to converse over the pulsating music. After two more plastic cups of Everclear enriched Kool-Aid, they were on the dance floor. Then in this room. And, crap, had they used protection?

She closed her eyelids and pressed a finger into her left eye, not that it resolved the lacerating pain.

"Your head hurt, too, wildcat?" The deep, sexy rumble of his voice sent tingles down her arms.

Her gaze snapped to his.

Concern smoldered in his deep blue eyes. "Here let me take care of it." He brushed aside her auburn bangs and laid a finger against her forehead. The pain fizzled into nothing.

What had he done? Maybe he was like her—not quite normal. Maybe he hid a few magical abilities. She'd searched her whole life to find someone else with *gifts*. Someone who could tell her why she had these talents. She sifted through her memories for clues to indicate he might be different. Nothing emerged. Disappointed, she concluded he must've hit an acupuncture point or something.

He rolled his wrist to view his watch. "I've got a rot-zee run in thirty minutes, but…" His tone dripped with suggestion. "I could be persuaded to miss."

"What's rot-zee?"

"ROTC. Almost all the guys in this frat are ROTC."

Idiotic question. Of course she knew what that was. She'd just never considered herself a soldier groupie. "What time is it?" She scanned the floor for her watch, but identified only his abandoned dark T-shirt and jeans on her side of the bed, and nothing of hers.

"'Bout five forty-five."

"I've got a chem midterm in two hours." She needed to get home to her reality pronto, not that she had any control over when she jumped worlds or where she'd end up. But this time the shift had to happen. She'd already bombed two quizzes and needed to pass this test with flying colors or risk a GPA slide, and losing her scholarship.

"Well…you could say we did some hard-core chemistry studying last night." He drew her tight to his chest and tucked her head beneath his chin. The heat of his body scorched her. His hoarse voice dropped to a whisper. "Sorry. That was cheesy."

She squirmed against him for freedom, even though her body begged her to melt into him. She froze when her butt hit his arousal.

"Don't go." The tremor in his voice tugged at her heart. With a finger on her chin, he turned her head and forced her to meet his gaze. "Please, stay."

His deep blues sucked her in, calmed her. And tempted her. Maybe last night had been as earth-shattering for him as she remembered it had been for her.

His lips touched hers. His tongue tickled the seam of her lips until she opened. Then the kiss deepened. Powerful, all consuming, aggressive. His hands plowed through her hair as he pulled her close until there was no space between them. He groaned when her fingers curled into his shoulders.

His touch made her head spin. It felt…right. Perfect. His hand trailed from the back of her neck down her spine, each touch light, not rushed. A soft moan echoed from somewhere deep inside her.

"God, you're amazing," he mumbled.

She smiled against his lips and kissed him harder. He cupped one hand around her breast, nibbled the sensitive flesh of her ear, and licked down her throat. She begged silently, *Please don't stop.*

A pounding on his dorm room door was followed by a feminine scream. "Who's in there with you, Matt? Shawn said you've got a party slut in there."

He pulled away and whooshed out, "Shit." He ran a hand over his head and rubbed his eyes.

"Who's that?" she asked as the passion haze cleared from her mind.

The pounding intensified. "Open up!" A loud thud whacked the door.

He scooted to the edge of the bed and massaged his forehead. He pushed to a wobbly stand and pulled on his jeans.

The moment he unlocked the door a perfectly coiffed blonde in a sorority sweatshirt shoved past him and pointed at Kat. "Who the hell is that?" The girl's thoughts bombarded Kat's mind, courtesy of her magical gift that worked on every person other than Matt. *Did you even tell her you had a girlfriend?*

Kat's heart cramped tight and then shattered. She managed to loosen the sheet and wind it around her as she slid out of the bed to stand. A desperate floor scan confirmed no evidence of her clothes.

Tears poured down the blonde's cheeks. "Matt? How could you?" She clung to him like a life preserver. The girl thought, *I love you. I was going to marry you.*

He mumbled something low to the girl, their familiar intimacy obvious.

"Get her out of here!" the girl screeched and then thought, *She's not even pretty.* Her high-pitched wailing burned Kat's ears.

A few guys crowded the doorway with too-curious leers. Matt pinched the bridge of his nose, and waved the guys away. He disentangled himself from the blonde and pushed Kat toward the door. "You'd better go."

She blinked against the sting of tears. Fury curled in her stomach. She narrowed her eyes, and slapped him. She gritted out, "May you never find satisfaction with another woman."

He paled and stepped back. He massaged his chest over his heart and whispered, "Did you just curse me?"

Like she knew how to do that. She tried to remember what she'd just uttered, but her emotions were running too hot to think clearly. At least he admitted belief in the supernatural. That didn't mean he had mysterious gifts like her, but it didn't matter. He was history.

Magical energy revved deep in her chest, warning of an imminent world shift. She spied her bra hanging off a lamp. Her pants lay near the mini-refrigerator. But fury and the terror of disappearing with an audience pushed her to forget them. She stalked to the door wrapped in the sheet, head held high and slammed it behind her. But she didn't miss Matt's bellow, "Did you curse me?"

Chapter Two

A DECADE LATER...

The timeless chords of a swing-era favorite filtered between the whirling vertigo in Kat Ramsey's brain. She attempted an eyelid crack. Light scorched her retinas. *Too soon for vision.*

She stumbled backward, bumping into a wall. With her eyelids sealed shut, she waited for her vision to stabilize.

It had happened again—the bizarre world shift. Moments ago she'd been modeling her newest online super-sale find in front of her full-length bedroom mirror. The strappy designer high heels worked with the spaghetti-strap black gown she'd purchased a year ago. Then her brain went dizzy and poof... now she was here, wherever here might be, in Otherworld.

The magical reality change wasn't time travel. Everything in Otherworld was the same year and similar technology, but it wasn't her home. Different people, different organizations, and slightly different politics.

The hum of many conversations at once registered in her ears as the chords of the familiar tune continued.

The imperfections of the music suggested a live band. She squinted. Her eyes burned, but she forced them to stay open. Nearby a horde of elegantly dressed women verbally one-upped each other and sipped at cocktails. The glut of jaw-dropping designer formal wear and sparkly jewels suggested a high-society shindig. Her dress was appropriate, even if it was off-the-rack.

Between one blink and the next, her eyes gave the thumbs-up on twenty-twenty again. A large banner along the far wall proclaimed, "Rose Center Juvenile Diabetes Benefit sponsored by Ryan Corp." The pamphlets lining the wall near her indicated this was the Natural Science Center in New York City.

Her heart raced, and she forced herself to swallow. Legs still wobbly, she continued leaning against the wall.

Pull yourself together. You've done this four times before. You'll get through this and go home. She focused on the physical act of breathing. Air in. Air out. Air in. Air out.

A waiter paused in front of her with a tray of glasses filled with white wine. Kat took one and thanked him.

She pushed away from the wall and sipped the wine. The rich, buttery flavor of chardonnay coated her palate and soothed her dry throat. "Mmm," she mumbled. *This isn't the cheap stuff.*

A horde of people crowded her, and she started to move away, but a male body smashed into her. The three-inch incline she'd forced her feet into was no match for a battering ram.

With lightning speed her unintentional attacker pulled her tight to his chest.

Thank God the wine didn't spill.

"Pardon me," a husky male baritone murmured. He didn't release her.

Startled to find herself walled in by the heat of a seriously intimidating, hard, male body, she backed up a step, forcing her savior to let go. "Thanks," she murmured.

One glance up and her lungs went on strike. This guy was built big. Uncompromising raw power in a six-foot-something package met her stare. A thin, sexy scar over his right cheek suggested he might not have had a pampered heritage. He was gorgeous. Forget gorgeous. He was utterly, mind-blowingly handsome.

The corners of his lips tipped upward into a seductive half smile. A smile she knew too well—Matthew Ryan.

"Are you enjoying yourself, Ms. Ramsey?" His gaze traveled to her chest and followed the line of the silver chain that disappeared between her breasts. His gaze darted up to hers. They scorched with the offer of sex and any carnal fantasy she dared conjure.

"Matt?" Sensation so intense it bordered on pain flooded her body, as if every cell had suddenly jolted to life. Her skin tingled, tight and hot.

"So you do remember who I am."

She wished she could squelch the flush that heated her cheeks, and the compulsive need to moisten her lips. "I'm not really enjoying myself so much. No." She took another step back, needing to distance herself from him. Her body might still light up for the bastard as instantly as the first time she'd met him a decade ago. But the memory of his rejection remained etched into her memory like a bad tattoo. Indignant hatred surged. She tried to catch his thoughts, but got nothing from him. Not even an impression of his emotions. He was still the only person she'd ever met from whom she couldn't pick up mental ramblings.

"No? Aren't you supposed to be polite and tell your host this is the best party you've ever attended?" His lips quirked upward into a grin, flashing a set of perfect dimples.

Ryan Corporation. Matthew Ryan. *Damn.*

She glanced around. Distractedly she said, "Looks like

a great party." Detailed male reviews of her anatomy, and women dissing every aspect of her appearance overloaded her brain. She massaged her temple against the seed of an excruciating migraine. *Focus,* she ordered herself. *Stop catching everyone's thoughts.*

The attention didn't surprise her. His presence commanded notice. Success and confidence seeped from his pores. As did power.

Her head pain pushed into the pulse-throbbing phase, and she winced, rubbing a spot on her temple.

"Headache?"

The cold clamminess of nausea had her swallowing hard. She forced a smile. She would not show weakness. Not in front of him.

You will not puke. "I don't often attend this type of event. I admit this wine is excellent." She tilted the glass to her lips. One whiff of the liquid's floral bouquet and she knew she shouldn't swallow. A childhood of ingrained social etiquette instructed she not spit the liquid back into the glass as her stomach demanded. Her Southern belle mother's horrified face swam in her brain. With determination she forced the liquid down. Her stomach clamped tight, warning her it would cope, but wasn't happy.

She chanced meeting his gaze—another colossal bad choice. Her nerves buzzed like a virgin facing her first kiss. She went for the wine again, not even realizing until it coated her taste buds.

The back of his fingers whisked across her exposed chest, briefly touching the chain. The delicate intimacy of the touch electrified all exposed skin. Wine caught in her throat, stimulating an immediate cough.

"Bit of glitter or something," he mumbled. The blue of his eyes smoldered when they lifted from her chest. He grinned as if he knew exactly the havoc his touch wreaked.

Kat wished she could come off as apathetic but her cheeks heated and she couldn't hold his gaze. Oddly, her head no longer throbbed. The nausea had also vanished. Usually it took hours when a crowd's thoughts overwhelmed her for the head pain to subside. There must be something to be said for distraction. Or, maybe Matt really did have magical capabilities.

She chanced meeting his gaze. The sexual invite in his deep blues shot her mind right into a scatterbrained fluster. A giggle almost escaped.

Was he trying to push them into the foreplay zone? Maybe this was his normal interaction with every woman he encountered. God knew his body was killer and his eyes promised satisfaction, something she knew he could deliver.

She'd never let him touch her again.

Close it down and objectify, she ordered herself. She focused to shut down her emotional grid as best possible, and on being professional, something she'd perfected after years as a veterinarian subjected to the gamut of wacky. Despite his self-assurance, a cold stillness rested at the surface. Gone was the enthusiasm of youth she remembered from their college one-nighter. Beneath his veneer, she sensed he masked a crouching deadly power. His was the gaze of a high-end predator, throwing its prey a seductive look, waiting for the perfect moment to strike.

And she was the prey. The thought doused any hint of lust like an ice-water splash.

"Not married?" His gaze skipped to her ringless left hand.

She lifted an eyebrow but refused to answer. Instead she asked, "You?" Her gaze fell to his left hand, also bare.

He flashed her a drop dead gorgeous smile. "It's been a while, wildcat."

"Not long enough," she gritted out. An unwanted vision from their long-ago night slow-moed in her brain. Washboard abs…hips pumping rhythmically just one beat too slow to meet the desperate need he created. Her body temperature escalated to critical overheat. *Stop it,* she ordered her mind. *The Sonora Desert will ice over before we're going there again.*

"We could do better a second time." His self-assured, yet stunning grin irritated her.

"In your dreams."

He opened his mouth to say something, but closed it again, and frowned. Was he taking her hint they weren't going there? And was that disappointment swirling in her gut?

A fiftyish man, with a handsomely tanned face and in-shape body, stepped in front of Matt. "I was just over there at the bar. I haven't seen you in a while, Matt. Nice party." He held out his hand.

Matt returned the handshake. "I hope you're enjoying the evening. Kat and I were just on our way to the dance floor."

Kat pasted on a pleasant smile. *Like hell I'll dance with you.*

The interloper's gaze dropped to her chest. His thoughts echoed loudly in her mind: *Fantastic boobs. Wonder who she is and where his girlfriend is. No surprise he's got a hard-on.*

Her eyes skirted southward on Matt, confirming the comment. Her face flamed hot. No hint of teasing remained on his face. No knowing eyebrow quirk. Just a mask of harsh control—unreadable and remote.

"Are you doing a speech tonight?" the guy asked Matt.

"Of course."

She phased out of their stilted, polite conversation. Years of pent-up resentment exploded in her brain. The unfaithful bastard probably seduced women on a nightly basis whenever his girlfriend left town. Her eyes narrowed his way, but his gaze didn't meet hers. She wanted to scream, *You have a girlfriend! Planning to cheat, again?* Anger revved, close to boilover. She threw a mental slap at him, but gasped when pain rocked her brain with the sensation of smashing against a brick wall. He blocked her?

What just happened? The two previous mental slaps she'd thrown landed her intended victim on the floor. Perhaps he really had used magic to clear her headache today and all those years ago. What was this guy?

His rebuke-filled gaze zeroed in on her. In a bored tone at odds with the warning in his eyes, he said, "I hope you're planning to donate."

"Of course." The other guy leered at her chest again. *Bet Matt wouldn't mind me borrowing her tonight.*

She stepped sideways, closer to Matt, creeped out by the guy's wolfish grin and the montage of X-rated images flashing through his brain.

Matt clasped her hand and said, "If you'll excuse us." He placed her glass on a passing waiter's tray and led her toward the floor.

She hesitated. Matt gripped her arm and propelled her through the crowd. He leaned close to her ear and whispered, "If you don't dance with me right now, that guy will read it as a yes to you spending the night at his penthouse."

She whispered back, "All he did was look."

"He's richer than God and fucks a different girl every night. I'm sure he'd be glad to add you to his dossier."

"Are you any different?"

His lips thinned. "Yes." Based on his closed look, that was as much as she'd get from him on this subject.

"Fine." Despite the resentment simmering in her blood, excitement thrummed through her as they neared the dance floor. Last year she'd won the national amateur Latin Dance championship. She loved moving on a dance floor.

On their way through the crowd, she glanced up at Matt again.

His stylishly disheveled black hair was just a tad too long, but not long enough to cover the small bad-boy silver hoop in his right ear. The earring didn't mesh with the expensive tuxedo tailored to his body. Over the years he'd retained the panties-dropper sexy. That in combo with the power he now radiated ramped him up to devastating.

And she wasn't the only one to notice. She gritted her molars in annoyance as most of the women in the vicinity stopped to stare. The only one who didn't seem to notice was Matt.

A random thought from a woman sneaked into her brain, *He never dances*. A man thought, *She looks like his first wife.*

He'd been married? She didn't like that thought. At all.

Once they reached the dance floor, he glanced down. "That guy wasn't your type, anyway."

Heart racing, she tilted her head back to look up at the man towering over her. "And just who do you think is my type?"

His gaze darted down to her mouth. Heat sparked in her belly, igniting the need to succumb to the white-hot connection between them. She didn't know what she wanted more. To slap his face publicly and extinguish this connection forever, or his arms around her to keep this connection burning hotly.

• • •

Your type? Me. Matt could barely believe the gorgeous redhead he'd tried to locate for a decade was here. And almost in his arms again. Kat Ramsey in reality eclipsed every latent memory of their one night, and every fantasy his brain had conjured since. They needed to resolve the problem of that zinger of a curse, which had rendered every encounter with other women to be a disappointment. But at the moment he barely cared. He was so hard that it might push him past the breaking point. He might just drag her to a dark corner and kiss her until the firecracker smoldering beneath the surface broke free. He wanted to hear her cry out his name in pleasure again.

"Smile. People are staring," he whispered.

A classic Sinatra song started, although the singer didn't do the vocal part justice. He slid his hand around her waist and stepped them into the slow dance. Her body was stiff, but she didn't trip or step on his toes. In fact, she moved so gracefully in sync with his lead that he suspected she'd had training.

A tense smile touched her lips. "I heard someone back there say you don't dance."

"It's been a while since I braved stepping onto parquet."

"I guess I should be honored then." She didn't meet his gaze.

"Perhaps I was inspired by the memory of a dance at an undergrad party long ago…" He trailed off.

Her cheeks flushed a darker red. "Don't get your hopes up for a repeat. Not happening."

"That might be a bit awkward, given our audience." She'd had most of his clothes off by the song's second refrain that night.

She shot him a squinty-eye warning that communicated if she could slap him, she would.

Shit. He hadn't meant to say that. He'd finally found her and now he was blowing it. "I'm sorry. It's been a long time since that night. I tried to find you, but you just disappeared."

She tensed and snapped, "You had a girlfriend. And, if memory serves, she wasn't pleased to find me in your bed."

Yeah, he'd handled the after part of that night miserably. That nightmare was probably right now replaying in her mind. He caught the gaze of a reporter whose too-keen interest in Kat had him saying, "We're just dancing. Lots of people are watching."

She glanced around and then smiled. “So…you don’t want a scene?” she asked in a soft, threatening tone.

Fuck.

“Kat…there are people here that will shred you. Please be careful. As long as you’re dancing with me you can avoid the sharks here tonight.”

She muttered, “Then you must be a great white.”

He managed to smile for their audience and twirled her around a few couples. There were too many eavesdroppers out here. Christ, he wished he could drag her away from all the scrutiny. To apologize for past pain and make new memories. Pleasurable ones. The hurt in her eyes made him feel as though someone punched him square in the chest. She’d probably hate that he’d glimpsed that vulnerability.

In silence they glided through a verse of the song. She was so damned beautiful. A strand of dark auburn hair mutinously curled out of the elegant twist, bouncing against her pale, slender neck. That rebellious strand was the only hint of disarray other than her residual blush. It begged him to release all her hair from the hairdo, as if that small act would liberate the hellcat he remembered from years ago.

The conservative, ankle-length, black dress she wore hid what he remembered had been a body designed to be touched. Her athletic figure filled out the dress in a way that pushed him to rip the thing off. And those long, tapered legs. He imagined pressing her against the nearest wall and driving into her. Those legs would be around his waist.

Cool off. This insanity over her had to be the damned curse. It guaranteed that he’d find her irresistible. After a decade he was desperate for what he’d experienced with her last time, and for what her curse denied he find with other women—repletion.

She cleared her throat and asked stiffly, “So, you own a corporation now?” Her body remained tight and she carefully maintained a few inches of air between them.

"Yes." He struggled to banish the Kat memory highlight reel currently playing in his brain.

"What type of corporation? What does it do?"

"We build parts for military operations around the world. We also build for drilling operations, especially underwater drilling."

"So you fuel the world's desire for destruction."

"We don't actually make weapons. Just the parts. It's a technology corporation," he answered on autopilot. Many hurled that accusation at him on a daily basis.

With a twist, he prevented them from colliding into a couple that had moved too close in an obvious attempt to overhear.

"Did you start this business on your own? It's not exactly what I'd imagined you doing."

"I inherited it from my father when he died."

She leaned back to look upward and gazed deeply into his eyes. Her deep green eyes widened. Softly she said, "I'm sorry about your father. But you don't like this work, do you?"

She'd pegged that one dead right. How could this woman whom he'd bumped into less than ten minutes ago discern what people who'd known him for decades hadn't guessed? Maybe her magical abilities extended to mind reading. He swallowed and smiled tightly. With a glance around he said, "I've turned Ryan Corp around since I started."

"Evasion. Okay." She glanced around. "What about ROTC?"

"I started my years in the army but then my father died and that changed. What have you been doing since…?" He cleared his throat. "For the past few years?" He forced a mental beat-back of the memory of kissing his way up the smooth skin of her inner thigh.

"I'm a veterinarian." Her body finally relaxed a bit.

"I can imagine you doing that. Do you like it?" He liked the feel of her small hand in his. And the flexing of her slim waist in his right hand. Would she taste the same? Her taste had tortured him. It had ruined him. His gaze zeroed in on her lips.

"Yes. I'm good at it. And it is rewarding."

The song ended. A small tap hit his shoulder. He held onto Kat's hand as he turned toward the source of the tap.

His PR director smiled apologetically. "I'm thrilled to see you dancing, Mr. Ryan, but we've got ten minutes. We need you to head over there to get the microphone adjusted and whatnot."

"If you two will excuse me," Kat said in an even tone. She slipped her hand out of his.

I can't lose her now. But, he had responsibilities. "It's been a pleasure, Kat. I'll see you later," Matt intoned. The heat in his tone promised her there *would* be that later.

She narrowed her eyes at him in answer and hurried away.

Matt blew out a frustrated sigh as he followed his PR director toward the podium. He watched Kat glide away, her movements graceful and sensuous. He wanted to warn off every male in the vicinity that looked to be fantasy fucking her. His control swirled at the edge of crazy.

He needed a drink. A good Scotch might help dull his need to stalk Kat and drag her into the nearest empty room. For an instant he considered tossing aside responsibility, ditching this event, and abducting Kat. He could think of several very persuasive ways to convince her to rescind the curse and guarantee both of them pleasure. *A drink…focus on a drink. Stop thinking about her and that spectacular ass.* The line at the bar looked to now be of a dissuading length. He tried to flag down a waiter. No luck.

Damn it, he was the CEO of Ryan Corp. They sponsored this event. He should get some perks, at least the drink of his choice whenever he desired.

As he maneuvered through the crowd, he avoided the many gazes vying for his attention. Those who hadn't found the opportunity to talk business with him at the office always tried at these events. They expected him to be easier to manipulate here.

He longed for a quiet night alone at his house in the Hamptons, with his dog. No press. No speeches. A nice Scotch and the most recent Formula 1 race on his widescreen TV. He hadn't come close to that fantasy in over two years. This was his third benefit in the past two weeks. He believed the causes were good and deserved whatever money could be raised, but he wished he could just give his own money and be done with it. Tonight was about putting on a good face for the corporation.

Kat now stood in a corner near the band with a new glass of wine. The arc of her sleek neck as she sipped distracted him. Little had changed when it came to the jolting physical reaction he had to Kat. Their chemistry was real. No other woman came close to what he'd shared with Kat, either before or since their one-nighter.

He grabbed a glass of wine off a passing waiter's tray, and sucked it down in one slurp. What a waste not to enjoy it, but he needed to dull his insane drive to be inside her, and only her, in every way possible. This was most likely a product of that damn curse. Staring at her now, he didn't know if he should beg her to rescind the curse or seduce her first. His southern hemisphere voted for the latter.

Speech. Think speech, he ordered himself. *Get your head on straight.* Control was the foundation of his life. Loss of it resulted in either idiocy or social death. His last idiocy spearheaded by his desperation to have a normal life, even if the bedroom lacked spark, ended in matrimony. What a colossal mistake that turned out to be. Lesson learned: a beautiful woman gifted in bed would do anything for the big diamond. Love, compassion, and even orgasms could be faked. What couldn't was being caught with a company intern's dick halfway down your throat.

Ever since his wife's infidelity and death three years ago, he refused to be ensnared again. Since none captured his attention for very long, and most belonged to the future billionaire-housewife club, the danger was low.

Kat, on the other hand, confused him. Her body wanted him, regardless of whatever resentment still simmered from the past. Her behavior indicated she had no interest in joining the billionaire-housewife club. And what was she? When he touched her to alleviate her headache tonight, he'd detected an energy buzz suggestive of recent use of supernatural power. The wind slap confirmed she had gifts, even if it had been a childish move. Exposing herself like that was dangerous. Years ago he'd searched for her on campus and at neighboring universities. He'd concluded she lied about her name and wondered if she was one of the seven dimension-hopping Pleiades witches. As the years rolled by, he'd discounted it. Now he wasn't so sure.

Within yards of the podium a familiar, gladiator-tall Scotsman blocked his path. Wasn't this turning out to be one hell of a night? He forced a polite smile while fisting his hands. "Who invited you?"

"I'm here to find *her*."

Chapter Three

Matt stared at Bryce Sinclair in stony silence until the jittery need to speak overwhelmed him. "Who are you talking about?"

Bryce replied low enough that no one nearby could overhear, "Ye've been avoiding my calls and emails. It's important we talk in private. Now. About *her*." Power oozed from him. That strength had kept him the leader of the Druides Society for almost thirty-five years.

Matt crossed his arms and glared. "I know no woman of mutual interest that we need to discuss."

Bryce frowned, revealing new wrinkles around his eyes. The grooves of his face etched deeper than the last time they'd clashed, eight years ago. "Come with me." Bryce pulled Matt to the periphery of the room. He spoke softly. "The Confirmation is days away. And we've got a bit of an issue."

"How is that my problem?"

A pained look pinched Bryce's features as if this was absolutely the last thing he wanted to admit. "We need your help. With her."

"I have no idea who you're talking about."

"All hell is going to break loose if we don't get this resolved." Bryce ran a hand through his dark hair, which lacked any hint of the gray expected for a man well into his sixties. Druid longevity was both a curse and a gift for those of the Sentry, the elite few chosen to protect the Pleiades witches.

"It's always the same shit. Something is always threatening the world or jeopardizing your wards. I'm not interested."

Bryce seesawed his jaw as if carefully selecting his words. "I've given you time. Now you need to step up. Get involved. Accept the fact that Quinn made his choice, and you being involved is your destiny."

"No. You left my father, your loyal lieutenant, to die. I could've healed him, if you'd given me a chance." His heart rate skyrocketed. Damn Kat for opening up the floodgate of hot emotion tonight. He forced himself to recognize his anger and not fall victim to it.

Bryce glanced around for eavesdroppers. His accent thickened, a sign of heavy emotion. "Ye were a kid with emerging abilities that were not entirely under your control. At best ye might've healed him enough to give him a few extra hours, not to mention you would ha' likely killed everything alive in the vicinity to garner enough energy, including yourself." He cleared his throat and swallowed. "Quinn didn't want that," he said, the accent no longer as detectable. "He wanted you out of that prison, and alive."

"You were only too willing to abandon the man that had been your right hand for three decades. He threatened your leadership and you jumped at the chance to get rid of him."

"Bullshite." He lowered his voice. "If he'd wanted my position and had been chosen by the ancestors, then I'd have gladly stepped aside. Dying was his choice. I granted a great friend his last request. I saved his son." A glassy look passed through Bryce's hard eyes. "It is high time for you to accept your legacy."

Legacy? Matt narrowed his eyes in a silent fuck-you.

Bryce squeezed Matt's shoulder. His tone gentled. "I need you to help me find a missing Pleiades. As you know, all seven must be there for the Confirmation in a few days. If not, the end of the world may literally begin from the resulting deity war. I've got her druid match, but he says she refuses to stay in this realm. I don't think they've bonded yet, though. Another source predicted that you would be the one to bump into her at some point soon." Bryce scanned the packed exhibit hall. "I felt a buzz earlier that suggested powerful magic. Did you detect anything? See anyone? A girl, perhaps?"

Matt's chest heaved with shock and then came to a full stop. Air refused to move through his lungs. He coughed. *He had her match?* Kat belonged to another druid? Not bloody likely.

Oh, hell no. Alarm squeezed his gut. He had no desire to become bonded to a Pleiades witch and get sucked back into druid matters. Bonding and druid shit was not on his list of lifetime to-dos. Besides, maybe she wasn't the girl Bryce sought.

But deep in his gut he knew. His suspicion about her was probably right. Only a powerful witch could throw a curse like the zinger she'd saddled him with. She had to be the missing one.

At the moment, though, he didn't have time to deal with this. He heard the music stop and his PR rep start her spiel about juvenile diabetes. He masked his inner turmoil and ground out quietly, "I have no knowledge of an unknown Pleiades. Ask someone who gives a shit about the world of the weird. I've got a speech to make."

• • •

Kat found an unpopulated corner near the orchestra that she deemed to be far enough away from Matt Ryan. Her hand trembled as she sipped wine, hoping the alcohol would lull her body back toward normal. Her pulse continued to thud through her ears and a roaring arousal made her uncomfortably hot. That combined with a hefty load of pissed off had her itching for a fight.

She wouldn't let Matt get her in bed. Not this time. She'd learned the hard way that he considered her good enough for an easy one-nighter, but nothing more.

Her curious nature, however, was intrigued that maybe, like her, he wasn't quite what he seemed. But curiosity didn't eliminate resentment. She had to avoid him for however long she was trapped in this alternate reality, which she hoped she'd leave soon.

In a daze, Kat followed everyone's gaze when the music stopped. They turned toward the raised dais close by. A woman she recognized as the one that spoke to Matt while they danced tapped at a microphone for attention. People crowded in next to Kat.

The pretty blonde said, "Let me now turn this over to our host this evening. He's been a strong supporter of this cause for years. Tonight he pledged a personal half million to the Foundation and challenges all of you to match that. Let's give a warm welcome to Matthew Ryan."

He calmly stepped up to the podium amidst the loud applause. Holding up a hand to halt the applause, he flashed a devastating smile guaranteed to make all the women want him. His supreme confidence and aura of authority were magnetic.

Beside her a woman thought, *I can't believe he murdered his wife.*

What? Kat had to bite her lip to stop herself from asking the woman for details. He killed his wife?

"Thank you all for coming out tonight." His deep, mesmerizing baritone washed over her. "I hope everyone is enjoying my liquor because I seem to be unable to get adequately hydrated. It's all right; I'll try to make it to the bar later." He waved off the blonde woman with a smile. Laughter followed.

He launched into a short, but powerful speech on the Juvenile Diabetes Foundation. She stared, mesmerized by the soothing texture of his voice, and not registering a single word he uttered. She shook off his persuasive influence and glanced around. Everyone appeared just as enthralled by his words.

A man behind her said, "He's a good speaker, isn't he? Persuasive. Are you going to donate?"

The woman next to her sighed with a moony look as if coming out of a trance when the speech ended. "I'm going to donate," she announced to no one in particular and drifted away toward the donation tables.

Kat turned back toward Matt. As the music resumed, he descended from the dais to shake hands with several powerful-looking men. His gaze captured hers over the tops of their heads.

She had to get out of here. Time to find a quiet spot to try to jump back to her real life.

Her mind whirled as she headed for an exit. Despite her resentment for Matt's past behavior, she didn't believe him evil. Annoying, devastating, and rude…yes. But a murderer?

Chapter Four

Kat needed to travel back to her apartment tonight. There were patients to see tomorrow. And dance practice in the afternoon. She also didn't relish being the recipient of a screaming litany from her boss when she missed work. At least she didn't have any pets waiting for her at home, having put down her cat a month ago after he lost his battle with kidney cancer.

She hadn't been able to control when she transitioned back to her normal life in the past, but there was always a first time. Right?

She darted into the restroom, intent on escape. Gossiping women and flushing toilets crowded the fluorescent-lit linoleum disaster. She backed out.

Noting there was no attendant at the coat-check station, she slipped around the reception desk. At the far wall of the cloakroom, she halted. "Come on. Please, let this weird evening end," she whispered to herself.

Nothing happened.

Warm breath tickled the hairs on her neck. A hand snaked

around her abdomen. Kat sucked in her breath and tensed. Every self-defense instruction she'd ever learned surged to the forefront of her mind. She prepared to yell, but the instant sound crested in her throat, a hand clapped over her mouth.

"Don't scream," a familiar masculine voice whispered in her ear.

Her body stiffened.

His hand released her mouth, but he maintained his opposite palm on the back of her neck. Chills skirted down her body.

She turned and met Matt's dark blue gaze. She resented the smug perception smoldering in his eyes. His jacket hung unbuttoned and the tuxedo tie undone. The cocky bastard expected a whole lot.

"Leaving?" he asked softly. His hand moved slowly from her neck to chin and gently stroked.

Pride demanded she leave. She would not allow this evening to end with them in bed and the utter humiliation of her being pushed out in the morning. Her festering anger bubbled to the surface. She jerked away from his touch but he caught her arm. "Let me go." She jerked again and he caught both of her arms, pulled her against his chest.

"We need to talk, wildcat," he said. "Just give me a few minutes."

Despite the coolness of his tone, she felt each heavy exhalation as it exited his body. His eyes blazed, excited. She should be frightened that he restrained her, but deep down she knew he would never physically hurt her. A fire of sexual need started in the pit of her stomach and quickly warmed every inch of exposed skin. Indignant fury warred with desire.

She said, "We have nothing further to talk about. *We* are in the past. Over." She slammed her eyes closed to hide her lust from his too-knowing gaze and to avoid being drawn into the seduction she knew lay in those sexy, deep blues. An instinct stronger than anger tempted her to wrap her body around him. She wanted every bit of the wild abandon she'd found with him before.

"Look at me," he ordered.

"No."

He pressed her against the wall and said hoarsely, "We are far from over."

She wiggled, needing to put some space between them. His heat and fresh masculine scent was all over her, making her abdomen clench with want. Anticipation and desire electrified her body. She fought to keep her eyes closed. If she opened them, he would suck her into his sensual vortex.

His palm curled around her lower jaw with a touch that was gentle but controlling. In a raw voice, he rasped, "Please, rescind it."

Her lids popped open. She asked with a deceptive calm. "Rescind what?"

His body tensed against hers.

She glimpsed the barely restrained desire eating at him. His gaze slid to the chain around her neck and followed its path down to where it disappeared into her dress. Evidence of his arousal pressed tight against her abdomen.

She swallowed, knowing she should tell him to back off, but couldn't voice the words through the desire clogging her throat. Defeating his iron control challenged her. Rational thought fled. She wanted to tempt him. To push his control over the edge. She arched her back until her breasts rubbed his starched shirt.

His breath hitched, then came in irregular pants.

She bit back a smile.

"This is insane," she murmured. She yanked her hands from his grip with surprising ease and fit them around the back of his head to draw him to her lips.

He murmured, "Not as insane as how much I want you."

And resumed kissing her. His hand shifted to fit the nape of her neck while the other cupped her butt and pulled her core to his groin. Her legs instinctually wrapped around his hips, pushing up her dress.

He groaned when she tangled her tongue with his.

A moan detonated from deep in her chest. Behind her head, his fingers expertly removed the few pins holding the French twist in place. He tangled his fingers in her hair and then molded them around the back of her head.

Shamelessly, she ground herself against him, desperate to be closer. The muscles of his back jerked when she dug her nails through the fabric of his tuxedo jacket.

He chuckled low. "That's the wildcat I remember."

His words pulled her abruptly from her passion free fall. She couldn't fight this attraction, but what remained of her functioning brain advised she stop. She was seconds away from begging him to quench the painful pressure building between her thighs. My God, she was on the edge of explosion just from a kiss. If that happened, she would plead with him to finish this right here in the cloakroom. Ten years of nighttime fantasies of him swam in her mind. *End this right now!* she ordered herself. She refused to become a repeat one-nighter, no matter how incredible the sex promised to be.

There would be consequences.

She tore her lips from his and lowered her head. She panted for control over breathing. What the hell was she doing? "We're not doing this again." She chanced meeting his gaze.

He cradled her chin—controlling, but not painful. The pupils of his eyes were so dilated that the blue was but a thin line. A tic worked furiously in his cheek. In that moment she saw a glimmer of the real Matt. The one her body burned to unmask. He clung to control by a thread. One little push and intuitively she sensed he'd explode. What would happen then she wasn't sure. But she didn't fear it. To the contrary, the mere thought made her knees tighten as she recalled the ferocious lover cradled between her thighs.

He rubbed the pad of his thumb along her lower lip. "Whatever this is between us isn't over."

Her voice came out as little more than a whisper. "It has to be. You're getting married." She wriggled to unlatch her legs from around him, but he had her pressed too tightly against the wall to escape.

"I haven't proposed to anyone yet."

"Well, you have a girlfriend…again."

He leaned toward her and whispered, "Not for long…"

Oh God, yes. Please kiss me again.

At the last second, he shifted to kiss the hypersensitive zone just beneath her ear. She groaned and her legs involuntarily tightened around his waist again.

"Please…not tonight," she whispered, wishing she didn't have to beg. But apparently her self-control flew out the window when this man touched her.

His breath was hot on her ear. "You're right. This isn't a good place, but you're not getting off that easy."

A momentary sting burned the underside of her left wrist where his thumb rubbed steady circles. Heat shot from her wrist directly to the junction of her thighs as if his hand was on the bare skin of those private folds, stroking erotic circles. She groaned and rubbed against him seeking something more. The sensation focused on the hidden nub.

"Come for me, Kat."

Sensation intensified. She whimpered and tangled her hands in his dark hair to pull him in for a deep, openmouthed kiss. Her body arched against him as her orgasm crested. His mouth buffered the moans that rose from her throat when her world detonated.

Oh my. She rested limply with her head against his chest

in his strong embrace. Her ear registered the loud thumping of his heart. His scent enveloped her and soaked deep into her pores where she feared she'd never eradicate him.

When her brain came back online, it quickly skipped from euphoria to humiliation. He touched her wrist and she climaxed? How utterly pitiful she must seem to him.

His rapid, heated breaths tickled her ear, but he held himself motionless.

"Please, let me go."

In a hoarse voice he said, "Reverse the curse. Please end it. Once I'm free of it, we can finish this without anything hanging over us."

She blinked up at him. "What curse?"

He eased her feet to the floor and kept a hand on her elbow.

She was grateful for his support because her jelly legs weren't on board with walking yet. She smoothed her dress.

"Don't play games with me, Kat. Do whatever you need to do to reverse it." He leaned in and gripped her arms.

"What are you talking about?" How could he be so calm after that? So seemingly in control and focused on her reversing something? She could barely wrap her mind around coherent thought. A curse? She recalled her parting words to him all those years ago. He must've believed it to be real. She hadn't intended such.

Beyond that…wow. That meant he hadn't been satisfied by any woman since her. Her heart squeezed. She owned a piece of this extraordinary man that no other could claim. That didn't mean she trusted him farther than she could spit. Even if she'd meant to cast a curse, she had no clue how to reverse it. Based on the stubborn set of his lips, he would push this until he got what he wanted.

She'd try mind coercion to get by him and leave, not that she expected it to work on someone so strong-willed. It worked on pets, if she could reach beyond their hospital-induced panic, and occasionally on some people. She announced, "I'm leaving. Please, let me go."

He scrunched his forehead, but didn't move. "What do you want from me in order to get rid of it?" His eyes pleaded with her to help him.

That meant none of her abilities worked on Matt. And she couldn't help him since she had absolutely no clue about curses. "I want to go home." She tried to back out of his clamp on her forearms, but he didn't release. His thumb stroked circles on her bare arm, shooting chills down her spine.

"Is there some guy waiting for you at home?" he asked hoarsely, pulling her close to him again.

Jealousy? From him? "Not that it's your business, but no. Unlike you, I don't cheat when I'm in a relationship." *As if she'd had a relationship longer than a first date*. No one she'd "dated" measured up to what she'd experienced with *him.* Damn him for ruining other guys for her.

"That's not fair. You tend to pop into my life at random. Why won't you rescind it?"

Desperate to distract him from the curse she asked, "What's that tat mean?" She pointed to the intricate woven Celtic-looking square tat on his right wrist. She remembered it from that night long ago, but never had a chance to ask.

He glanced at the mark. "Mistake of youth."

"We all make mistakes." For a few seconds she allowed her gaze to roam over the angles of his face, memorizing each detail from the strong chin to the arched dark eyebrows. The thick ridges of his biceps and wide shoulders strained beneath the dress shirt. Men in her world just weren't made like this without CGI-screen magic. Her body cruised rapidly into overheat again.

"Hey, you can't be in here!" a man yelled from the cloakroom entry.

They jumped simultaneously. Matt released her and put himself between her and the middle-aged man in a maroon jacket adorned with a museum name tag.

The attendant stormed toward them. "What are you doing in here?"

"She needed her coat."

"Where's her ticket?" The attendant held out his hand.

Matt patted his jacket and produced a ticket. "Here's mine. She lost hers."

Tingling spread in her body. *Oh, no.* A world shift was starting again. "I've got to go." She rushed past the attendant in a jog toward the exit.

"Kat, stop! We're not done."

She pushed out the front doors and staggered into the side of the building when vertigo teetered her world. One couple huddled together against the bracing wind while waiting for their car to pull up to the curve. A valet helped an elderly lady into the backseat of a limo. Kat stumbled along the sidewalk with a hand against the side of the building. The familiar whirling sensation flowed through her head. Then it stopped. She hadn't left Otherworld. Yet.

Matt would be behind her. Right now she couldn't handle another confrontation with him. She darted down an alley, hoping not to run into anyone, and slipped into a recessed doorway.

Now what?

She rubbed her itchy right wrist. Her fingers traced a raised area. It burned. This called for an immediate evaluation. She rotated her wrist into the beam of ambient light from a streetlamp. A raised pink outline of a symbol rested on the underside of her wrist—three ovals that intersected in a triangular symbol. It wasn't a tattoo but more of a scarred burn. A brand?

Oh. My. God. She rubbed at the area and then scratched

the mark, desperate to erase it. But it remained. Now her skin was red and sore around the reliefed symbol. This must've been how he'd managed to create the sensation of touching, and then made her come. Witchcraft? Or something else? Something evil?

Her heart beat too fast. She couldn't breathe. She stumbled against the concrete alcove, dizzy. *Breathe.* With her hands on her knees she breathed deeply until the light-headedness passed.

He's not evil. She believed that on a fundamental level. But he did have his own magical, or at least supernatural, abilities. Could this mark be a curse or hex? Her mind whirled with possible curses he might cast onto her in retaliation for the one he believed she'd cast onto him. Why would he do this now, and not years ago in undergrad? They hadn't had much time together in undergrad. Or motive.

A curse? She focused on slow breathing for a few seconds when panic spun her mind again. *Be rational. Don't freak out.*

It's not a curse. She'd researched witchcraft over the years in a desperate attempt to understand her bizarre mind-reading ability and world-shifting problem, coming to no conclusion on what she was. But she'd learned enough to know this brand wasn't a curse. Curses didn't involve physical marks. She didn't recall anything about magically appearing marks other than in fictional novels.

Exhausted, she leaned her head against the door. Regret lodged itself deep in her gut. Resentment had prompted her to push away her one chance to speak with someone who might be able to help her understand her magical abilities. Aside from that, she'd just cast aside the only guy who truly knew how to make her body sing. The cold, rational side of her brain commended her for applying the brakes.

But she wanted to see his wild blue eyes smolder again as if he was three seconds shy of detonating.

No you don't! You did the right thing. He'd devastate her again, if she gave him the chance. She might not survive a second time.

She pulled the chain free of her neckline. Her fingers traced the familiar lettering: Matthew Zacharias Ryan. The only reason she'd worn these for nine years was to give them back to him, if they crossed paths again. For years she'd dreaded seeing him again, but another part of her needed that confrontation. She just hadn't counted on turning into a flustered mess when it happened, and completely forgetting the tags.

She'd had them since she'd shifted to him, a year after their disastrous one-nighter. Matt had been imprisoned—blinded, tortured, and his body damaged. She'd released him from his shackles, and then as he stood, she'd lost her balance and clutched at him, accidentally grabbing the tags. The chain broke and she'd instantly shifted back to her real world.

For years she'd wondered if she'd freed him from a failed military op. And worried that he hadn't gotten out. Nightmares about him hurt and imprisoned still frequented her dreams, more so when she was stressed from work. She'd never let the memory of him slip away.

Apparently he had gotten free and done just fine for himself.

The whirling resumed in her brain, and gut instinct told her she'd be jumping back to her world any minute. She dropped the tags. She'd do better next time she bumped into Matt. There would be a next time. She had questions about the mark on her wrist. And then there was their undeniable attraction. He was right. They were far from done.

• • •

Matt raced outside seconds behind Kat. He scanned up and

down the street, and ran to the nearest alley. Residual magic tickled his senses. She'd disappeared again.

He swore, slapping the stone wall of the museum. The wild side of his brain roared in anguish that he'd lost her again. Why hadn't he ripped her panties off and taken her to sate the teeth-clenching desire he'd lived with for ten long years?

He was an idiot. That's why. And too focused on the damned curse. Now she was gone. Again. And for who knew how long. Before the cloakroom attendant interrupted them he'd planned to invite her home. To go slow. Maybe take a day…hell a couple of days, maybe even a month to explore what they had.

That realization surprised him. He never took women home. He usually went to their place or took women to the hotel he owned downtown. With Kat, though, he had a bizarre desire to invite her into his private sanctuary. To see her in his bed, on his sheets, and in his bath.

This should freak him out. Should. Yet, he was calmer than he'd been all night since she'd shazamed into his life again. Absently he rubbed the Sentry tattoo on his forearm. If she was Pleiades as he suspected, then as a druid, especially a Sentry, casual sex with her was forbidden for him. Good thing he wasn't bound by the rules of that group anymore.

But her safety did concern him. The Order Lutomalifacum, who relentlessly hunted the Pleiades, would find her in no time. He'd planned to never get entangled with druids or Bryce again, but for her… Damn it. He was cornered.

He yanked the smart phone from his pocket and dialed. Maybe she had a residence in this dimension, somewhere Bryce couldn't find. He knew someone who could ferret out the location of almost anyone.

His call went directly to his brother's voicemail. "Eli, I need a background check and a current location on a person." Although they'd been separated at birth, they'd both become covert operatives. He a Ranger. Eli in British intelligence. As ex-MI6, Eli was spooky in his ability to get intel on anything. He was one of the few people Matt trusted. And he was a druid. Eli hadn't recanted his vows, and he respected Matt's decision to remain inactive. "Her name is Katherine Ramsey. That's Katherine with a *K*. I met her ten years ago when I was at Yale, but not since then. This is personal and confidential. Let me be crystal clear on this. That means not one fucking word to Bryce about this."

He ended the call and entered the museum. He glanced through the open doors at the benefit still going strong as the cords of a familiar swing number filled the air. He had no reason to return. There wasn't a single woman among the crowd of beautiful possibilities that could ease this need. He also didn't want to be cornered every few steps to discuss political or business bullshit.

He may be good at being CEO and enjoy the power that came with success, but he never wanted this life. When his stepfather unexpectedly died two years ago without leaving an heir, obligation made him leave the life he craved as a Ranger. Covert ops gave him a sense of rightness. His twin was lucky that he could continue that life.

Thinking about Quinn brought on a resurgent sense of responsibility toward Kat. Quinn had constantly made him recite the five druid axioms. Number five echoed in his mind. *Protect the Pleiades unto death.*

For Quinn, he would confirm Kat was Pleiades. If so, he'd get her suitable protection. She would need it soon or the OLM might find her and kill her.

But he needed her to confide in him that she was a Pleiad. He may no longer consider himself druid, but he wasn't about to be the first to reveal the not so normal side of himself to anyone. That was self-preservation one-o-one.

He drummed his fingers on the valet desk while waiting

for his Porsche. He rubbed the inside of his left wrist, which only intensified its subtle burn. Confused, he inspected the area. A pink triangular brand of three intersecting ellipses marked his wrist. He recognized the symbol as Celtic *triquetra* but couldn't remember what it signified. Vaguely he recalled feeling a raised area on Kat's wrist.

Shit. He'd marked her.

Quinn had warned him long ago that he'd mark a woman when subconscious desire collided with destiny. If this was such a mark, why hadn't it happened years ago?

Destiny's a bitch with no mercy, Quinn's voice answered in his mind. *She'll choose her own time.*

With this permanent mark he could track Kat and remind her of him at will. It also meant her coming apart in the cloakroom probably had nothing to do with his use of the Voice.

If destiny planned a renewal of his druid status, then it would be disappointed.

Chapter Five

Kat pushed away from her dance partner after her third stumble in five minutes. “This isn’t going to work, Riley.” She bumped against the wall-length mirror of the studio after another stumble on Riley’s foot.

Riley cocked his hip and rested a fist on his waist. “I can’t believe you forgot your dance clothes. You can’t move right in clogs and scrubs.”

“The surgery on that Rottweiler ran late, and I didn’t have time to go home. I see you had time to change out of your scrubs.” She scanned his red Lycra shirt v’ed open to his navel, exposing his tan, shaved chest, and skintight black pants. No straight man would be caught dead in that much rayon and spandex. His spiky blond hair and magnetic personality rounded out an extraordinary package. They had become friends at one of his wine-tasting soirees when she found herself a minority of one. Riley had whirled her into a rumba in his dining room and discovered her latent gift for dancing.

“Am I going to have to find a new partner? Regionals are in a few weeks.” Riley pursed his lips.

She raised her eyebrows. As if a new partner could catch on to his complex choreography moves as fast as she could.

Riley rushed out, “All right, sorry. I just…come on, Kat. What’s up with you? You’re never this forgetful.”

She faced her reflection in the wall mirror, unsure how to answer. Tracing her neck where Matt’s mouth had touched twenty-four hours ago, her mind once again replayed last night’s cloakroom encounter. She may never see Matt again. Or, perhaps not for another ten years. How many opportunities would she really have with a man like that?

You are in trouble, she thought. *He’s trouble. For you.* He turned her brain to mush and her body into someone she didn’t recognize. But this morning she concluded she needed to see him again. He had unusual abilities and might be able to help her understand hers, especially the world-shifting problem. She just had to be careful not to end up naked and used.

She jumped when Riley whispered in her ear, “Earth to Kat. Where are you?”

Her gaze met his in the mirror. “This isn’t going to work tonight. I’m sorry. I know we need to practice.”

He sighed, and then ordered, “Stay there.” He walked to the sound system and scrolled through his iPod. The chords of her favorite salsa surrounded them.

She smiled as he returned.

“Lose the clogs. You’ll be less likely to trip barefoot.”

She kicked off the shoes. He twirled her into the familiar steps of a salsa. She focused on the moves. As always, she was careful to avoid Riley’s thoughts. His chaotic brain usually played images of men in leather outfits with holes and straps in areas that left things hanging out.

“Relax,” he suggested. “What’s going on? You okay?” He stumbled for an instant, his face shifting to super inquisitive.

Oh, no.

He slowed their pace. “It happened to you again, didn’t it? The time-travel thing?”

No use denying it. “The astrologist I saw a couple years ago thought they’re detailed, albeit extremely realistic, dream scenarios or past-life experiences. That means I don’t actually travel anywhere. I certainly don’t change times.” *You’re such a liar,* she thought. It was real. She’d been wearing Matt’s dog tags for years.

Riley twirled her into a series of spins and then back to facing him. “Where’d you go this time?”

She spun away from him into a solo hip gyration exhibition.

He caught her back to him. “Come on. What happened?”

She threw him a stubborn look and danced in silence for a while.

Riley shrugged. “Fine. Don’t tell me what happened. But, I want you to come to my meeting this week. We’ve got a special speaker coming. She talked to us last year, and I think she might be able to help with your disappearing problem.” The song ended.

“Is this one of your Wiccan things?”

“Shhh.” His gaze darted to the few people trickling in for the group class starting soon. He whispered, “I keep telling you that you’ll fit in better with them than me, what with your little…problem.” He stopped and jiggled her arms. “God, you’re so tense.” He leered at her. “You need to get laid.”

Kat rolled her eyes. Leave it to Riley to think sex fixed everything. “Is this you offering to be my booty call?”

He briefly granted her a body scan and shook his head. “Nope. But if I was going to swing your way, you’d be my first choice.” He laid his hand on her cheek. “I know you got hurt in undergrad. We’ve got to get you past that. Not every guy’s a shit. I’ve got this friend, if you’re interested, that I could hook you up with. I can’t say he’d be in it for the long haul, but he’d be fun." He dropped his hand and stepped away with a grin.

"Is this another one of your friends that's interested in an experimental walk on the other side? That last guy you set me up with spent our entire date checking out the other guys in the restaurant and not me."

"Okay, I won't fix you up. For now. Hey, how were those fuck-me pumps that came in yesterday? Do you think they'll work to hook a hot date?"

She'd already proved they *worked.* Her mind replayed the coatroom highlight reel. "They're strappy…and way out of my budget."

"So they're smokin' hot. Excellent. Keep 'em. You need to embrace showing off your stellar body in some arena other than dancing if you want to hook Mr. Right." He moved away to undock his iPod. He grinned over his shoulder at her. "Actually, who wants to be tied down to Mr. Right at our age? We're young and all we need is a hottie with skills."

She put on her clogs and grabbed her handbag.

"Maybe you'll find someone at Friday's meeting. I'll pick you up at eight." His phone dinged. "I gotta go. Got plans tonight. I met someone last weekend who's got a body to die for." He kissed her on the cheek. "I love you and you're worrying me right now. Let's try again tomorrow after work. We've got that exhibition on Saturday that we need to prepare for."

She squeezed his hand as he pulled away. "I love you, too."

She headed for the bathroom at the back of the studio, needing a break before she went home. Inside she wiped away the mascara under her eyes, then leaned in closer to the mirror. *Shit, more lines. I'm definitely getting old.* With her twenty-ninth birthday looming she was tired of the failed internet dates. Why, then, continue the online-dating torture?

She liked the thought of longevity. Of a life partner. But

she had yet to meet anyone she trusted enough to foray into bed with since Matt. Ten years. *Had it really been that long?*

Damn him for ruining her for other guys. She absently traced the swirly edges of the raised brand on her wrist while staring at her reflection.

A disorienting lightness entered her head and she stumbled into the wall.

Oh God. Not again.

Chapter Six

Matt's finger froze on its way to deactivate his penthouse security. The blinking red light put Matt on instant alert. He glanced down the dark hallway, then back to the digital clock on the alarm panel, which read 10:05 p.m. His day of nonstop meetings had been hell, especially since his mind was trapped in a nonstop personal fantasy fest with Kat Ramsey as the star. Then a three-hour, seven-course dinner at his mother's house had put him in a sour mood.

Low grumbles from his TV emanated from the rec room. He lived alone. No one other than his housekeeper was allowed inside. She never watched TV, and he barely did.

He unlocked the hidden gun vault beneath the hall table to retrieve his 9 mm. As he stalked silently down the hall, he opened his senses to detect the auras in the air around him. The intruder was a druid. A familiar one. And likely reclined on his sofa in his rec room sucking down his last Guinness. Damn it.

He tucked his gun and cell into his overcoat pocket. As he rounded the corner into the rec room, he said to his brother,

"Yep, thought you'd be finishing off the last one. A little consideration for once might've been in order. Did you even consider that I might've been saving that?"

Eli granted him his classic like-I-give-a-shit smile before taking a hefty swig from the bottle. He closed his eyes in appreciative bliss. In his perfect British accent he said, "You can afford to buy more."

"You want to change lives and do this thankless shit? Just give me the green light and I'll fix that scar so it doesn't cross your entire face, just a little something like mine. Imagine, all this can all be yours."

Eli ran a finger over the scar that ran diagonally from his forehead, across his nose to chin. It was the reason he'd been pulled from MI6 missions. Too memorable. "I've become attached to this. It's nice not to be identical. There's also no way I'm spending Fridays with your mental sister and your mother. Not to mention those boring-ass PR parties and business bureaucracy. You can keep it."

"Allison is your half sis, too. She's not that bad. And Mandy is your mother. You should actually meet them at some point."

"How is Allison doing? Any recent hospital trips?"

Matt shook his head. "She's still struggling." He wished he had the miracle cure for her anorexia and depression.

"I still wonder why Quinn only negotiated to free one of us from that life. Why he'd leave you in the hands of Mandy and that psychotic asshole Grant Ryan…" Softly he added, "If you'd have let me I would've killed the old bastard for you. For what he did…"

Matt shrugged. His stepfather. Any time he dwelled on the abusive prick, years of repressed rage screamed for freedom. The asshole left a tornado of devastation in his wake when living, and continued to fuck with him from the afterlife. Thank God Matt wasn't blood-related to the guy.

His mind moved to his bio-dad, Quinn, who had appeared when he was about ten, and spent years secretly tutoring him to use his druid talents, right up until Quinn's murder eight years ago. He'd begged Quinn to take him away from the Ryans, but Quinn always denied him out of deference to some deal arranged with his mother. Matt never understood. He vowed if he ever had a child trapped in that type of situation, he would do anything to get him out of it. Even so, he was grateful for every moment he got with Quinn.

"Why are you here? Did you find any information on Kat?"

"Sort of. This will seem mental, but I'm on assignment from the Big B."

Matt swiped the longneck out of Eli's hand and took a deep swig. He closed his eyes in bliss. "Damn, that's good." He handed back the bottle. "Does Bryce still think we hate each other?"

"Yeah. But I think he suspects we're not really on the outs."

"He just can't leave me alone this week. I'm not going to have a sit-down with him."

Eli shook his head. "Not about that. He wants intel on a Pleiades. Katherine something or other. He thinks you've got her chained in your bedroom. Is she the same Katherine you asked me to research?"

Matt shook his head. "I don't know. Did you get any information on her yet?"

Eli shrugged. "I've been busy."

"Doing what? You're retired and from what I can tell you've become a professional couch potato."

Eli flipped him off. "This Katherine thing is way too coincidental. She's probably the same girl. But I didn't even need to check your place. No way would you get *involved* with one of them. That is even too stupid for you."

Matt's neck heated. "Yeah."

"If I gave a shit, I'd be jealous. I think Bryce likes you better than me. He's obsessed, really. Every meeting he corners me to ask about you. He wants you back. Bad."

"Probably because his current shaman sucks." Matt sank into a plush chair.

"The new healer isn't that bad. He's just a little green." He clicked through a few channels.

"He's that bad, huh? Does Bryce still think he can make you into a shaman?" Matt snagged a Dorito from the open bag on the coffee table.

Eli grumbled, "He just doesn't get that I don't have your level of healing ability."

Even though he wasn't hungry, Matt couldn't resist another chip. As he crunched, he asked, "So, now that you've confirmed I don't have her, what're you going to report?"

"Do you know where the girl is?"

"No."

Eli grunted and took a swig of beer. "So, how bad you got it for her?"

Matt scowled.

Eli was silent for a second, then laughed.

Matt's face burned. His twin couldn't read minds, but knew him too well. "Bad enough. I was looking forward to that beer tonight."

Eli continued laughing to the point that he snorted. "This is too good. You get her in bed yet?"

"None of your goddamned business."

"She was that good, was she? You're screwed." Through laughter Eli managed to choke out, "No pun intended." Eli suddenly sobered up. "Shit. That's why Bryce is always up my ass about you, isn't it? Are you the one he thinks is her destined?"

"Look, I may have been with her once a long time ago,

but I'm sure as hell not her destined. It's not like that." Matt sighed and threw his head against the sofa cushions. "I ran into her last night at that benefit event. I think she's probably the 'Katherine' that Bryce is searching for."

Eli clicked the TV onto mute and sat up. "You're shitting me. I mean, I theorized but…fuck."

Matt shook his head. "I'd still like you to do research and see if you can find her here. If you can't, then she needs an identity to throw the OLM off her trail. She's in serious danger. Can you set that up? I mean, why not use those MI6 skills for some important hacking?"

"I can try to put something in play for her tomorrow, if I come up with nothing. It won't be airtight, given that she's already on the OLM radar. Can you get a picture of her?"

"Maybe," Matt said. He closed his eyes and relived the memory of Kat in the cloakroom.

Eli chuckled.

Matt's fantasy paused. He scowled at a very amused Eli. "What?"

Eli's smile didn't waver. "Deny it all you want, but it looks like the gods have plans for you. Bloody big plans."

"The gods can go to hell for all I care." He was in trouble. Eli was right. He pushed off the sofa. "I'm going out to buy some more beer."

• • •

Kat pushed her eyes to pass through the rebellious nonfunctional phase fast, not that it worked. Stinging cold wind and spitting ice rain tore into her scrubs. Her knees folded against the too-familiar vertigo, landing her hard on the damp sidewalk. Water soaked through the thin cotton scrubs where her legs hit the concrete. The bus stop sign a few feet away offered five ways to get cheap Broadway tickets.

New York. Again. At night.

She stumbled upright and into a lean against a stone building. After the standard period of disorientation and eye burning, she swiped rain from her eyes and gazed around. Now what?

An icy gust speared through her soaked scrubs. Full-body shivers racked her to the point her teeth clacked together.

A large hand snaked around her arm and clamped tight. "Come with me, whore of the devil. Or I'll kill you," a man ordered.

Her heart pounded so hard that she feared she'd have a heart attack.

The man towered over her. Maniacal hatred shimmered in his dark gaze.

"What do you want?" she asked. *Rape? Mugging?* She tugged against his bruising grip. She couldn't pick up any thoughts from him other than streamlined motivation to kidnap her.

He laughed low, menacing. "I am the gateway to your salvation."

"What do I need saving from?" *Keep him talking.* At least then she wasn't being dragged into an alleyway.

"Shut up, witch." He wrenched her arms behind her. She heard a plastic zipping sound and then her wrists were secured. Tight. With a rough jerk he forced her to stumble up the slick sidewalk beside him by gripping her bound wrists.

"Let me go." Had he seen her sudden appearance and assumed her to be a witch? Or was that some sort of slur? She slammed on the brakes and refused to walk. He raised her bound arms behind her back. The excruciating pain in her shoulders forced her to bend forward and move wherever he wanted. She tripped and lost a shoe.

He caught her against him before she face-planted onto the wet concrete. "Walk," he ordered.

"My shoe…"

"Fuck the shoe." With a curse, he thrust her body outward, slamming her into the side of the building. Her head bounced against the stone in a mind-numbing ricochet. Dizziness gave way to excruciating head pain.

He shook her, activating a vicious mental spin. As he leaned in close she smelled coffee and cigarettes on his breath. He gritted out, "Shut up and move, or I will kill you. They don't care if I bring you in alive or dead."

"Let her go," ordered a male.

She blinked through her double vision toward the source of that voice. Matt. Her heart jumped, and her stomach did a small crazy flip. Complete and utter confidence surrounded Matt. Ice-cold anger reflected in his gaze.

Relief flooded her.

"Or you'll what?" asked her attacker.

Matt's grin promised pain. This was the predator she'd sensed yesterday. The volatile danger radiating from him sang to every one of her senses and reassured her.

"Have you come to save one of your pets?" Her captor moved her to stand in front of him as a shield.

"I am not what you think," Matt replied.

"We know about you. And her." Her captor wrapped her neck in a headlock and pressed a gun to her temple.

Renewed shivering shook her body. Her gaze didn't leave Matt while her mind whirled with regret and shock. *I'm going to die.* Her captor choked her neck tight. She couldn't get in air. Panic rose sharp and fast. She gasped and choked. Her mind whirled.

Matt raised his hands to shoulder level. In a low, mesmerizing voice he said, "Kat, take a breath. Breathe for me, baby. Nice and slow." He addressed her captor, "You don't want to shoot her." He took two steps closer.

"Get out of my way."

"Put the gun away," Matt said in that soothing tone. He took another step forward.

"If you take one more step, I'll blow her brains out. Now back the fuck up." Her captor subtly eased his hold around her neck.

She sucked in air.

Matt jumped forward to grip her captor's gun hand, folding the weapon away from her head and into her captor's chest. Matt slammed his elbow into her captor's nose. The force of the hit pushed her captor slightly backward. He released her. Momentum slammed her onto the sidewalk. Pain streaked through her at the jarring landing. Dazed, she watched Matt fight. The freezing water seeped into her clothes.

Matt didn't release the guy's gun hand, keeping the weapon pressed tight with its muzzle aimed into her captor's chest. Then he gripped the back of her captor's neck to pull him down while he kneed upward into his face several times, never releasing his grip on the gun, which was still pressed tight to his chest. There was so much blood that her captor's face was barely visible.

Matt kneed him in the face once more and asked, "Are there more of you?"

"Fuck you," her captor grunted. Then he pulled the trigger, which released the bullet through his own chest. His body slumped to the ground. Dead.

"Damn it," Matt cursed. He peered up the street for a few seconds. Then he patted down the body, recovering a brutal serrated knife. He knelt next to her and popped apart her wrist binding with the knife. "Are you okay?"

She couldn't stop shaking, her teeth chattering. So cold. Her gaze locked on his face.

He put his arms around her and pulled her close. If he hadn't been nearby…oh God. She bit back a sob as the reality of her almost death crashed in. She burst into tears, and sobs racked her body.

Pressing her face against his solid chest, his fingers slid through her hair and over her back in soothing motions. “You’re okay now.” His hand slid upward over the nape of her neck, his fingers slowly massaging.

The sobs diminished. Kat wanted to stay right here. Safe. Warm. After a few residual sobs, she murmured against his chest, “I’ve never seen anyone die like that. I’ve never seen anyone killed.”

“I didn’t have a choice. One of us had to die. It wasn’t going to be me or you.”

With the back of her hand she swiped moisture from her eyes and then pulled her head away from his chest. Her uncontrollable shaking was lessening. She should say something meaningful or maybe even grateful, but her mind remained a mishmash of frozen fear.

Sirens echoed in the distance. He glanced up the street. “We’ve got to get out of here. Gunshots in this neighborhood means someone called the police. Do you think you can stand?”

She nodded and took his hand to help her up. After a few wobbly steps she rubbed her forehead against the headache. The world shifted from doubles to singles. “My head hurts…” Darkness engulfed her mind.

Chapter Seven

Matt lunged forward to catch Kat before she smacked onto the concrete. Christ, she was soaked and freezing. Maybe she had a concussion. He placed two fingers on her neck. Thank God, she had a weak pulse. He shot a quick bolt of healing energy into her to stabilize her.

He needed to get her out of this rain to somewhere private where he could use his healing ability to fix her injuries, but not his apartment. Eli would face off with him over doing *the right thing*, which for Eli would be calling Bryce. Then he'd lose her to the druids. No one would take her from him now that he'd gotten her back.

His office was two blocks away. Two very long blocks, but still a better option. He swiped her purse off the ground but couldn't locate her other shoe. Sirens echoed in the distance. He jogged away from the scene with her in his arms.

On his way out of the elevator at his office building, she moaned and demanded, "Put me down."

"Are you sure? You fainted."

"I did not. I do not faint." She pushed against his chest to glance around. "Why are we inside?"

He smiled at her baffled expression. "You almost conked your head a second time when you went down."

"I can walk. My head feels…fine, which is weird. It really does feel absolutely fine now."

At least the quick healing session in the elevator had worked. He liked holding her. A lot. And didn't want to release her. She squirmed. Reluctantly he lowered her, but kept a hand on her arm until she stabilized.

She stepped away, putting a few feet of air between them. "Where are we?"

"The Ryan Corp office building. It was close." His gaze dropped to the scrubs plastered to her body, outlining every perfect curve.

She crossed her arms and looked around the hallway lined with expensive artwork chosen by a designer years before he'd become CEO.

"Aren't you at least going to thank me for saving your life?"

She uncrossed her arms. "Yes, of course. Thank you. I'm sorry." A myriad of emotions passed through her eyes before she said, "I keep imagining what that guy planned to do."

"He can't hurt you anymore."

"I know." She shuddered and shadows passed through her eyes again. "How did you find me there?"

"I was at the corner store."

She mumbled, "Strange coincidence."

"Yeah." The improbability of that *coincidence* had churned in his mind ever since he'd spied her being dragged up the street. It suggested she might be linked to him, if she'd just shifted into this dimension. This would be the third time she'd shifted directly to him. And if she was a legitimate Pleiades witch, then that might mean she and he were… Nope, he wasn't finishing that thought. No thoughts of destineds right now. There was just him and her…and now. And some unfinished business about a curse.

He said, “Let’s get you out of those clothes and warm you up.” His gaze dropped to her pebbled nipples. “I can tell you’re still freezing.”

“I’m not sleeping with you.” She crossed her arms over her chest, obstructing his view.

“That suggestion came from you, not me.” He stepped close and slid his hand around the back of her slender neck. “You had quite a trauma. But I could be convinced it might be a good idea.” *No this isn’t a good idea.* He knew better. But everything about this woman challenged and then seduced him into an irrational need to touch her.

She gasped when he swept his thumb up and down the indentation of her neck. She stiffened. Indignation flared in her gaze. “I won’t deny I’m physically attracted to you. I don’t know why, but you are exactly the kind of guy I have decided it’s best I avoid.”

“Kiss me.” *Reassure me you’re alive and okay.*

Her gaze snapped to his lips. A flush stained her cheeks.

He leaned in close and whispered hoarsely, “Kiss me, wildcat.”

Her fingers dug into the collar of his coat and tugged him down to her level.

A ripple of shock went through him when her lips touched his. He pressed her backward against the wall. With a groan he teased her lips apart. He’d meant to tempt her, but his control rapidly slipped away when she moaned and her tongue tangled with his. She slid her leg over his to notch his hips firmly between her thighs in a desperate way that signaled she sought relief from the same need consuming him. They kissed furiously until breath ran short and they paused to draw in air.

“More,” she requested.

"More what? This?" Matt hooked his arms beneath her legs and positioned the straining length that pressed insistently against the fly of his jeans against the junction of her legs. He ground her back against the wall and kissed her again.

She cried out as she absorbed his thrusts. His erection slid in mind numbing friction against her.

He kissed his way down her neck. Slowly his mind registered her soaked clothes, her slight shivering which could be from cold or desire, and the crusted blood on her forehead. He stopped.

"What?" she asked. Her arousal-drugged gaze raked his face.

Don't look at me like that. Please. He was having a hard enough time trying to do the right thing. "You need to get dry. Out of those clothes."

"Exactly. Out of my clothes." Her hand caressed his ass as she kissed along his jaw.

Fuck.

He lowered her to the ground. And stepped away.

"Really?" she said. "You started this, and now you're backing off?"

"You had a nasty head bump and could have a concussion." He knew she didn't have any problem with her head. He'd fixed that. But doing this with her right now wasn't right, not when demons might be chasing her into this.

Her eyes slid to fury, shooting sparks. She looked disheveled, untamed and so sexy. He wanted to attack her again. *Do the right thing, which is not this.* He paced ahead of her to his executive assistant's office while repeating that mantra in his head. His assistant was a serious gym rat. He pawed through her drawers until...bingo. He held up yoga pants, T-shirt, and sneakers.

"Isn't this invading her privacy, and stealing?" Kat asked

tightly.

"I'll reimburse her." He frowned at the crusted blood on Kat's forehead and matted into her hair. "How about you take a shower? Wash off the blood." *You could invite me to join you.*

She touched her head and nodded.

He led her through his office to the adjoining bathroom.

"Thanks," she said curtly and slammed the door in his face.

• • •

Kat gazed at the door, knowing Matt hadn't budged from his sentry post on the other side. She was so frigging furious that he'd started what he had and then left her desperate. Every inch of her skin burned hot like she'd been sitting too close to a furnace. She was tempted to yank open the door and demand he give her the relief she needed, maybe even in the shower. She'd never done anything like that in the shower.

Oh God, she was in so much trouble. One hint of encouragement from him and she'd be the one tearing off that sexy black overcoat and peeling off his jeans. *Remember, you shouldn't sleep with him.* She would never be free of him if she did. Being honest with herself, she'd never really escaped the memory of their one night a decade ago. Her only hope was to resist him and pray that her obsession with him passed. Maybe she could condition herself not to respond like a cat in heat every time he touched her.

Right.

The man was too sexy. He had great lips. Very defined, very masculine. And he knew how to use them. With a shudder, she imagined those lips on her whole body. *Stop it.*

She stared at the bruises on her forearm from her would-be kidnapper. Had Matt not appeared, that creep would've killed her. Probably painfully. Now Matt wasn't just the guy who she bumped into every single time she bounced into Otherworld, but was her honest-to-God hero. And didn't that just make her stomach somersault and her heart squeeze.

As if on autopilot, she twisted on the shower, peeled off the damp scrubs, and washed. Suddenly she needed to erase the memory of her attacker's touch. She scrubbed. And scrubbed. Her skin pinkened from the vigorous loofa wash. After she'd used the entire bottle of body wash she leaned against the shower wall and let the hot spray scald her overly sensitive skin. She could still feel that creep.

Get out, she ordered herself. In a daze she pulled on the too-large yoga clothes and brushed her hair. She stepped out of the bathroom and forced herself to meet Matt's brooding gaze. Had he been out here the whole time?

With a push away from the wall he said, "Come." He led her into the spacious corner office and asked, "Coffee or tea?"

"Tea sounds good."

He disappeared into an adjoining room. She wandered to the windows. What a spectacular view of the city lights at night. Turning, she took in a wall-sized painting of an almost empty sky hanging behind a polished wood desk. A huge white board filled with scribbled words and connecting lines took up another wall.

He reappeared and handed her a steaming cup, waving at the white board. "It helps everyone—employees and clients—know what we stand for and our goals. We update it all the time." He sipped at his own cup and gazed at her, his expression cool.

She sipped the tea. Too hot.

God, she wanted to feel him surrounding her again. She was desperate. *Desperate.* She couldn't stop staring at his mouth. Images of him kissing her, touching her, swirled in her mind. Sweat gathered between her shoulders. She didn't know if she moved to cover the distance between them, or if he did, but within seconds their cups were on the desk and his mouth was on hers. His teeth scraped and tugged at her lower lip until she opened for him with a relieved groan. Fire swept through her. She gave herself completely to his control, wrapping her arms around him.

His hands tangled in her damp hair and held with a tight, almost ruthless grip. The bite of pain increased her need for release. The tips of her breasts ached as they rubbed against his shirt. With a groan he deepened the kiss. She slid along his thigh, seeking pressure to find relief. She fumbled at his jeans fastening.

"No." He tore his mouth from hers. He released her hair and gripped her hands to halt their motion. "Not like this. Not on a post-death-threat high."

Denial roared in her brain. "You're saying no to me… again?"

"We are not doing it like this. Not when I won't know if this is your fear chasing you. When we do this, wildcat, it will be about you and me. I'm not going to fuck you now just so you can blame me tomorrow for taking advantage of you."

He was rejecting her? She'd practically flung herself at him and he rejected her. Twice. She studied his stubborn expression, torn between scratching his eyes out and begging him. She would not beg. She'd only hate herself later. Humiliation fed fury. "Fine. Hand me my purse and call me a cab."

• • •

"Where will you go?" Matt realized he fully believed her to be a Pleiades witch. But according to Bryce she was *lost,* whatever that meant. Either she meant to be "lost" from the world of druids like him, or she really didn't know anything.

The not knowing seemed impossible. All the Pleiad women were so carefully guarded. So diligently trained from birth for their roles. Sentry druids committed their lives to protecting them, and sometimes died adhering to that vow. These women didn't just get lost.

She squinted furiously at him and searched the room. "Where's my purse?"

He watched her dart back into the bathroom, and then into his secretary's office. Damn it, why couldn't she be normal? A superhot veterinarian without an ounce of goddamned magic. Regardless of how much he wanted to throw her on that couch and fuck both of them senseless for about a week, it'd be wrong.

When had he grown a conscience when it came to women and sex? He raked a hand agitatedly through his hair and said, "Kat, you're exhausted. You whacked your head pretty hard and I'm worried you could have a concussion." *What a crock of bullshit.* He'd resolved all injury from the head bump. "Stay here tonight. On the sofa. You need someone close by to be sure you don't go into a coma from a concussion. In the morning we'll talk over breakfast. Then I'll drive you home."

Her gaze darted to the door. Forlorn fear skittered through her eyes before her gaze slid back to his. "It has been a really long day. Maybe I'll just rest a few minutes."

Oh, hell. She might really be in the not knowing category of lost. That meant she had nowhere else to go. An orphan in an alien world. He couldn't imagine that level of fish out of water terror. His respect for her notched itself to the highest level. He retrieved a blanket from his closet and handed it to her. "I've got some computer work, if it won't bother you."

She accepted the blanket and settled onto the sofa without another word. Within minutes she was out.

They needed to talk. He had to figure out what she knew and get her protection. That OLM Acquisitions bastard wouldn't be the last. The group had acquired a very good Sighter that could read for future continuum disturbances and dimension hops.

For a while he watched the steady rise and fall of her chest. He looked down at his shaking hands. He could withstand torture and pain. He'd been trained to kill without a second thought. He could sew his own skin when knifed or shot. Nothing shook him of his calm.

But he couldn't stop his hands from shaking out of the need to touch Kat. To reassure himself that no injury remained. And just to touch her beautiful skin. He wanted to wrap himself around her and hold her tight until she woke up. His need for her ran soul-deep. Far beyond what any silly curse could conjure. He'd tried to forget her for years, but now admitted he'd never be free of her.

Chapter Eight

Kat blinked awake, taking in the unfamiliar office. Matt's office. Her shoulders hurt, but she wasn't sure if it was from sleeping on a couch or from having it wrenched by her almost kidnapper. Images of her death terror and then utter humiliation from last night crashed into her brain.

Without sitting up she squeezed her eyes shut. *Come on, I want to go home. Now.*

Nothing happened.

"Finally, you're awake," Matt announced. "I ordered us breakfast."

She sat up. "Wow. You, me, *and* all the Yankees can eat." She blinked at the mounds of food on the coffee table—pastries, eggs, fruit, breads, jellies, and were those mini-boxes of cereal?

He sat on a footrest on the opposite side of the coffee table. "I didn't know what you'd like. So, I got a bit of everything." He smiled earnestly.

"This is very generous of you." She stared at the offerings, unsure if she should go for fruit or carbs.

"Try the apple strudel. It's from a German bakery just up the street. They sell out by six thirty every morning." He sliced a generous piece and put it on a napkin. "I never share. So, consider this a high honor." He held it out to her.

She accepted the strudel. "Thank you." She bit into the pastry. "Mmm. That really is delicious." She finished it and smiled. "I think I've found a new favorite food."

He flashed that smile that made her heart race. "The bakery's owner reminds me of my grandmother. More?"

She shook her head and snagged a banana. "That stuff is delicious, but deadly."

"I got this for you." He sliced another piece and moved around the coffee table.

Seeing the mischievous sense of purpose in his gaze, she scooted over on the sofa and then stood. She backed away from him as he advanced, effectively backing herself into a corner.

"Open up," he ordered.

She opened and bit in. So delicious. Once she'd finished she narrowed her gaze on him. "That wasn't fair."

"Maybe not, but you liked it." He resumed his seat on the opposite side of the coffee table.

Laughing, she retrieved the napkin he'd handed her earlier and dabbed her mouth.

"You missed a bit." He leaned across the table and wiped a finger against the corner of her mouth. He licked his finger. "Amazing." His gaze smoldered.

She busied herself with pouring juice into a plastic cup. "Would you like some?"

"Sure."

As they both sipped juice, her imagination kicked in. She imagined slowly unbuttoning his shirt and pushing up the T-shirt beneath. Then she'd trace every muscular dip down to his pants. Would he be commando, or was he a briefs guy? The yoga outfit suddenly felt uncomfortably hot.

"How do you like being a veterinarian?"

She shook off the fantasy. "It's got its ups and downs. My boss is a bit of an ass. I plan to change clinics as soon as my contract is up in two months. But I like my clients and the pets always make it worthwhile."

His gaze changed to angry, almost to the point of deadly. "Why is your boss an ass?"

"Likes to yell all the time. Yells at the staff, yells at the doctors. He's charming to clients. It's disgusting how much his clients love him. He's very successful, though."

"Why did you elect to work for him if he's like that?"

She snagged a bagel and spread cream cheese on it. "Oh, he's all charm in the interview. He conned me into thinking I'd found the perfect workplace. Once I signed the contract everything changed, but by then I was locked in. How about you? You seem to be very good at what you do, but why don't you like it?"

Matt's eyebrows shot upward. "You're the first to accuse me of that. How did you guess?"

"You got a certain look when I asked before that clued me in. Why aren't you in love with your job? It looks like you've benefitted well from it."

Matt shifted on the footrest and glanced away from her. "It wasn't my first choice of careers. I stepped in when my father had a heart attack and died. There was no one else. My mother would've gladly destroyed the company piece by piece out of repressed rage for my father. He… Let's just say this place reminds me of him every single day, which isn't a good thing."

She reached across the coffee table and gripped his hand briefly. "I'm sorry. You could step down or sell."

Matt shook his head. Sadness passed through his gaze momentarily. "There's no one else that could hold this place together. No one else that gets my vision."

She raised her glass of juice. "A toast. To doing what we must to survive."

He slowly grinned. "To future endeavors."

Her face burned, knowing without a doubt that meant her. Her mind wandered to her personal dilemma of world changing. He still wanted to *talk*. Really talk. That meant explanations. Crap. She didn't think she could handle that yet. Also, being in continued close proximity to him would definitely end in more humiliation since her willpower in his presence registered about zero. She couldn't handle another rejection. Then again, maybe he'd heat things up so she'd get that first-time shower sex. *No, no, and say it again…no!*

But she had wanted to talk magical abilities with him. He might actually understand her mind-reading ability or world-hopping dilemma. Then again, maybe he wouldn't. And just maybe he'd consider her nuts, which would lead to more humiliation. Did she trust him enough to brave that discussion? No.

What she needed was research. On him. And on her world-jumping problem. Once she had some facts, then she'd feel more confident braving that conversation on magical issues.

"Thank you for all this food. If you'd excuse me, I need to use the restroom. Do you have my purse? I'd like to get something out of it."

He walked to his desk and removed her purse from where it hung off the back of his desk chair.

"Thanks." She fast-walked to the bathroom adjoining his office. Hadn't she seen another exit to this hallway?

Yes. She pushed through into what she could only assume was his secretary's office. She couldn't dart out without leaving a note.

She grabbed a pen off the desk and quickly jotted a note

on a sticky pad: *Matt- Thanks for the clothes and breakfast. I'm sure we'll bump into each other again. -K*

That sounded silly. Now she wanted a rewrite, but in a few minutes he'd figure out she left.

On the elevator she rifled through her purse, counting out sixty-two dollars and some change.

As she rode away in a cab, a stab of guilt made her turn to watch Matt's office skyscraper disappear behind them. Maybe she should've had that chat with him.

• • •

Matt gazed sightlessly out his office at the early morning panorama. His mood ran about a hundred miles south of foul. He shouldn't have let her out of his sight. Now he didn't know if she was running around the city unprotected, or if she'd shifted back to her other dimension. He hadn't detected the buzz of magical energy suggesting a dimension hop, but he wasn't sure he would recognize it.

He fingered the mark on his wrist, wondering how it worked. Long ago Quinn mentioned he could track whomever he marked, but Matt didn't remember how. And he'd never call Bryce to ask.

He massaged his forehead against a headache. For the thousandth time his mind tortured him with the image of Kat coming apart against him in the coatroom, and that little hitched breath in the back of her throat. He recalled the flush on her cheeks and drugged satisfaction in her gaze, even if she had hidden it within seconds. He should've at least taken her back to that high last night. Hell, he should never have stopped her when she almost ripped off his jeans. Why had he caved to good intentions when he might not get another chance? He cursed.

"Excuse me, Mr. Ryan? I didn't catch that. Do you need

something?" His secretary laid a stack of mail on one side of his desk.

"I could use coffee." Matt schooled his features to stoicism as he turned to face her.

"Of course. Cindy Ellison called before you came in. She requests you call her at this number by ten this morning. Also, your mother called and wants to confirm you're still to be counted on for the benefit next Thursday. She wanted to remind you that you promised dinner again with them tonight. She said something about a special friend of Allison's you needed to meet." She placed two pink phone communication slips on his desk. "Don't forget the interview and photo shoot with that news magazine this afternoon at the beach house."

He said, "Please confirm the heli to depart at noon, then."

"There was this odd sticky note on my desk that looks like it's for you. I'll get your coffee and confirm the helicopter departure." She held out the note.

Matt grabbed the note. His heart raced as he read Kat's message. It wasn't an *it's-over* note, but it also wasn't a promise for anything more either. The note didn't clarify if she was gone or still in this dimension. Damn it.

When his secretary returned minutes later with coffee he asked, "Did Eli call?"

"No."

He grabbed his cell phone off the desk and dialed Eli. "What did you find out about her?"

Eli replied, "I'm not going to play games about this girl, Matt. I told you Bryce has got a hard-on to find a girl named Katherine. He's pressuring all of us. Hard. I still think your Katherine is one and the same."

Matt fell into his desk chair, which groaned in complaint. "She really could be one of the Pleiades." It was more of a statement than a question.

"I couldn't find jack shit on Katherine Ramsey with a *K*.

She doesn't exist. Bryce ordered everyone to scout for her. I do mean *everyone*. When we find her, we bring her to him. He doesn't often give us the details on the whys of what he demands. Bryce's craze might make sense if she is a Pleiad."

Matt spun his chair to stare out the window and consider his options. "I need you to hack into security footage from my office. Then email me the camera footage of her exiting the building this morning."

"Her as in Katherine Ramsey? You had her in your work building today? What. The. Hell?"

"This is between you and me. I rescued her from an Acquisitions team last night."

"Oh, Christ. Is she okay?"

"I healed her. She's a little shaken up, but fine. Then she ditched me this morning right after breakfast. I don't know if she walked out of here or shifted away. I need the footage. After you send it to me, corrupt it."

"Can do." Eli cleared his throat. "You need to speak to Bryce about this."

"This is none of his business."

"All right. I've got your back. I'm just warning you. Bryce's got a burr so far up his ass about this that if he finds out you harbored her, he will go nuclear. I also feel obligated to say if she is a Pleiad, then your helping her had better be to get her protection, and not one of your booty calls."

"Just send me the goddamned footage." He hung up.

• • •

Online research at the library showed the date here was the same as at home. History wasn't exactly the same, although Kat found some similarities as she scanned internet news. She wondered if she had an identity in this world and Googled herself. A few hits came up, but none were her. She typed in the webpage of her clinic in North Carolina and discovered the staff was completely different. At least she wouldn't have to worry about running into herself.

She Googled Matt. A photo of him on the cover of a celeb magazine propelled her heart to a sprint. The top button of his white dress shirt was undone and his black tie hung loose. That half smile and six-o'clock shadow sent liquid fire throughout her body.

She skimmed the article and a few other interviews. They confirmed he'd built a powerful company, but she only cared about his personal life. He'd been linked to a handful of women. But only one marriage a few years ago, which lasted six months before he and his wife separated. His wife committed suicide weeks later. How sad. As much as it hurt to realize he'd loved another woman enough to marry her, she wondered why it'd been so short. This was the history of a man not big on commitment. He'd be perfect, if she was looking for short-term.

What is wrong with you? She wasn't looking for any *term*. She just wanted to go home. There was nothing related to Matt and magic online, not that she'd expected it.

Someone in this world or hers would be able to make sense of what she was doing here and how this reality change was possible. She punched through a few web searches, finally getting helpful hits with "research on dimensional travel." A theoretical physicist at Columbia University popped up with a few publications on dimensional time travel. Based on the number of blog sites with his name, and the pages of debate, they must be highly controversial papers. Columbia was in the city. Close and quite convenient. She jotted down the professor's phone number.

An hour later Kat approached a student absorbed in a thick textbook, reclining on the stone steps of an academic building. Apparently, the kid was immune to the bitter wind that tore through his clothes. Shivering, Kat pulled the cheap wool coat she'd purchased at Goodwill tighter, jealous of the kid's tolerance of the cold. How she missed the South. They never got more than a dusting of snow, and never wind that could spear through any cloth barrier.

"Where's the physics department?" Kat asked the student.

The kid gazed at her with a vacant, somewhat stunned look. He removed his earbuds. "You talking to me?"

"Yes. Where is the physics building?"

He pointed. "Over there. Pupin Hall."

"Thanks. Sorry to bother you."

Heat enveloped her in a cocoon of warmth as she stepped into Pupin Hall. She ran up several flights of stairs to make it into Professor Yossi Webb's office two minutes late for their designated meeting, and opened the door to a modest room filled with books piled haphazardly on shelves. The floor was cluttered with stacks of papers and notebooks that, if it was organized into a system, could only make sense to the owner of the office.

"Hello. Anyone here?"

"Yeah, have a seat," said someone on the floor behind the desk. "Found it." A hand waved a well-worn piece of yellow notebook paper over the desk before a head appeared. Clear, dark eyes peered at her through small wire-frame glasses.

The man's graying black hair was pulled into a striking comb-over to swirl from the back of his head to the bangs.

"Who are you?" he asked.

"Katherine Ramsey. I called this morning."

"Oh, right. You had some questions on dimensional travel. Are you a reporter?" His cold tone conveyed distrust. He crossed his arms in front of his chest.

"No, it's a personal question. Are you Dr. Webb?"

"Yes." He glanced impatiently at the wall clock. "I only have a few minutes before I've got to teach." He shuffled through the notebooks on his desk.

"Dr. Webb, is it possible for a person to move between realities? Like live in two different worlds?" she asked.

His motion halted. He closed the notebook he'd been thumbing through and peered at her over the top of his reading glasses. "Why do you ask?"

"I just need to know what you think about it. Theoretically, of course. I'm writing a book."

He rose from his chair and moved to the office door. He pointed a finger out the door. "Look, Miss, if you're a jumper, you need to get out of here. Please."

"What do you mean *a jumper*?"

"They got me once. Held me for a week until they finally believed I didn't know one. You wouldn't believe what they did to me. I'm only a physicist. Most of my theories are based on the story of this Australian lady I met six years ago. She vanished within days of when I met her and I never heard from her again. I think *they* got her."

"What are you talking about?"

He closed the door and rested his back against it. He took a deep breath, then continued in a hushed tone. "A jumper can move between dimensions."

"There might actually be people that can do this? Wow. Did she say she was the only one?"

He pushed up his glasses and gazed at her for a few seconds. "She suggested there are others."

"Where could I try finding this Australian woman?"

"Like I said, she disappeared. I met her on a trip through Costa Rica at a hotel."

"Why do you think this woman could move between dimensions?"

His eyes took on a faraway look. "I theorized that something in this person's genetic makeup allows for the person to move in such a way. Perhaps, with disciplined training and experimentation it could be a tool to be used to learn about dimensions. I started looking for jumpers. But…"

When he didn't resume after a few seconds she prodded, "But what?"

"*They* found me and I've been trying to forget about the whole thing since. Are you a jumper?" He cocked his head as if fascinated, but there was a distinct tremor of fear in his tone.

"Not that I'm aware of. I was just curious about your theory. That's some pretty good material, though. Can I use it?"

He visibly relaxed. "No. They'll go after you."

"Who are you talking about? Who will come after me?"

"The OLM. Order Lutomaleficum. They're a fanatical fundamentalist Christian sect. There's nothing sanctified by God in what they do, at least in my opinion." He looked at his watch. "I've got to be going. I'm sure you can find your way out." Looking distracted, he pulled open the door and scurried away.

She stared at the spot he'd vacated. She was a jumper, and there were others like her. For the first time since realizing she was stuck in this alternate dimension, relief washed over her.

A trip to Costa Rica was out of the question. Her mind snapped to Matt. Maybe he could point her in the direction of the right people, other magical people. Her mind seesawed between fear she couldn't handle the desire he evoked, and her need for knowledge.

She was so distracted in her thoughts as she headed toward the building's exit that she almost hit a tall, dark-skinned man. She mumbled an apology.

He grabbed her arm. "Come with me, Ms. Ramsey. We need to talk."

She put the brakes on and glared at the physically powerful man towering over her. He reminded her of her would-be kidnapper from last night. Today, there wouldn't be a Matt to save her. "Who are you?"

Uncompromising black eyes silently communicated hostility and insisted submission. He was dressed to blend in with a forgettable black overcoat and jeans. A skull-fitting fleece hat camouflaged his hair.

Softly, he ordered, "Please come with me. Your life is at stake."

Her gut insisted she flee. *Now*. His attitude didn't convey the knight-in-shining-armor persona. His mind was nothing but determination. "I don't think so. Let go of me."

"Come quietly, or I'll make it hurt." The man's grip on her upper arm turned bruising.

The muscle monster dragged her beside him toward the exit from the physics building. She stomped the heel of her sneaker into the top of his shoe.

He grunted and yanked her close. "Listen, you little bitch, one more move like that and I'll carry you out of here. Alive or dead. They don't care."

On instinct, she focused her power of suggestive communication and surprised herself by confidently ordering, "Let. Me. Go."

The man's eyes glazed, and he released her. She slapped the heel of her hand against his chin, knocking him away from her. With a pivot she ran for the exit.

A noise like a racquetball hit sounded behind her. A second later, dust scattered around a hole inches above her head in the wooden door. He was shooting at her!

Glancing back, she saw the man emerge from the building behind her, lock onto her, and follow. She sprinted to the far side of campus, slipping a few times on the slick walkways. She heard the suppressed pistol fire again at close range. Razor-sharp pain sliced through her upper right arm. She grabbed the area and darted between the buildings.

She halted in the alcove and pulled open a side door.

Pulling her hand away from her arm, she saw blood. A lot of blood. She spied a women's restroom and dashed inside. Beneath the coat and shirt, there was a wide gash. This would require a hospital visit. For now, a wad of paper towels stuffed under her sleeve was the best she could do.

Exhaustion and weakness powered through her. She collapsed on the floor. Without thinking she touched the brand on her wrist, the one from Matt that she forgot to ask him about yesterday. The familiar dizziness started again.

Chapter Nine

The frigid wind tore into Matt's body while he scanned Shinnecock Bay below. The arctic chill thrashing across the cliff didn't faze him. Whitecaps tossed chaotically in the water beneath a gray-green horizon that threatened more of the atypically early snow. Waves crashed relentlessly against the rocky shore.

He dreaded the impending interview, and had been tempted to call it off when he found out the reporter was running late. But the company needed good PR. The only reason he had agreed to this interview was the recent media frenzy speculating on his impending nuptials. To complicate matters, the media accused him of a sordid affair with one of Hollywood's hottest starlets, whom he'd never met. He needed to show his corporate persona.

He leaned into the wind, enjoying its bite. But it didn't cool his frustration. Between his worry for Kat, who he now knew to be somewhere in the city unprotected, and a board meeting rife with infighting, it'd been a horrendous day.

To top it off, he had received an email from Bryce saying,

"We are going to talk. Name your time and place."

Eli must've relayed his suspicions about Kat, or Bryce coerced him into revealing them. The right thing was for him to turn Kat over to the druids for protection, when he found her again. He would find her. He smiled and massaged his wrist. He could try to track her when she reentered this dimension. But, he wasn't so sure on the turning-her-over part.

A sidelong glance caught view of his estate manager, Sam, approaching. The deep grooves of his face were drawn into a pinched frown. He clutched Matt's forgotten winter coat tight to his body as he fought the wind to make it up to his cliff perch. Sam had handled the thirty-acre Ryan estate for two generations of Ryans. He was proudly training his daughter to follow in his footsteps, not that Matt expected the old guy to retire until he fell over dead. Thank God that would be a long way off.

"Mr. Ryan, the reporter and her photographer have arrived. We prepared the sunroom for the interview." He held out the coat. His glower suggested not taking it would lead to an argument Matt wouldn't win.

He shrugged on the coat and followed Sam back to the house. "How did Milo's vet visit go this morning?"

Sam grinned. "The old geezer tried to bite the vet again. Your dog has got red flags all over his chart, but this new vet was fresh out of school. He thought he was better than anyone before him." Sam chuckled and shook his head. "Conceit of the young."

"Did Milo hurt someone?"

"I had to muzzle him since they couldn't get the nylon thing on him, and then they took him to the back. The vet looked a bit haggard when they returned him to me. I swear that dog looked proud, but they didn't mention any problems. They did suggest sedating him next year. I think they mentioned that last year, too. Milo got an overall good bill of health."

Matt laughed. "He's a tough boy. Wants life to be on his terms."

"You're right about that. Milo will outlive us all."

Matt smiled and squeezed Sam's shoulder. "Thanks for taking such good care of him. He's…Milo has been with me through tough times. I'm sorry I didn't have time to take him today."

Sam nodded and wrapped his arms around his chest, bracing against a new blast of wind. "I almost forgot. There's something wrong with the helicopter. The pilot doesn't think it's safe to fly in the storm that's settling in. He said it's going to take a while to repair it, but expects it to be ready tomorrow morning. Shall I arrange a car to take you back to the city this evening?"

Matt sighed. "No. I'll stay until tomorrow." They both entered the house.

Sam took Matt's coat. "Very good, sir. Dinner at eight?"

"Let's do the kitchen tonight. The formal dining room only feels right for company." He pulled out his cell and texted his mother to let her know he wouldn't make it for dinner.

• • •

The interview progressed as expected for nearly thirty-five minutes when sensation ripped through the mark on his wrist. Kat was close. His heart directed as much blood as possible to his groin. Subtly he shifted, hoping the pressure against his zipper would deter his erection. The move backfired, and only worsened the pressure of confinement.

Through the glass wall of the sunroom, Matt caught sight of Kat's small body as she fought against the wind and falling snow, stumbling toward his front door. She clasped a black wool coat tight around her. Auburn hair whipped in the wind, the snow contrasting beautifully against its rich red. Just as he was about to jump up to help her, she made it to the sidewalk, and safely on her way to the front door. Watching her, he was so transfixed that he completely missed the reporter's question.

"I'm sorry, could you repeat that?" he asked politely.

"During the past few years you've reportedly been linked to many famous women around the world, most recently with Cindy Ellison. Were these affairs real, and if so, do you plan to stop them when you get married again?"

"I have no plans to marry any time soon." Matt leaned back in the suede plush chair and gave the young reporter what he hoped was an inscrutable stare.

The reporter prompted, "In Ms. Ellison's TV interview last week she clearly indicated preparations for a wedding were in the works."

He needed to squelch Cindy's little campaign to drag him down the aisle. "I have not proposed to anyone recently, and certainly not to Cindy."

The reporter remained silent, clearly expecting him to expound. When he didn't she asked, "Do you mind being labeled an international playboy?"

"I don't believe I am." Matt lifted an eyebrow, daring her to push him on this line of questioning.

Momentary unease crossed the reporter's face.

Matt wondered if Kat was inside the house yet. He shifted impatiently. Would this interview never end? He had more important business. Like determining if one beautiful redhead was a Pleiades, and convincing her how much he'd make it worth her while to rescind the curse. He was tempted to use the Voice and end the interview.

The reporter clicked off her digital recorder and closed the notebook in which she'd pretended to take notes. She stood, smiling with satisfaction. "Thank you, Mr. Ryan, for taking the time to speak with me. The photos we got earlier should prove to be brilliant."

"You're welcome. Sam will show you out." He stood to shake her hand, but his eyes strayed toward the front of the house. Kat had to be inside by now.

• • •

Kat gazed at the giant man who answered the front door. On instinct she knew Matt had to be nearby. Every time she jumped into Otherworld she bumped into him. "I'm sorry for the intrusion, but I need to speak to Matt Ryan." She gripped the bannister tight when dizziness caused her to stumble. She'd bounced between Matt's world and hers within a minute. Between the energy drain from two jumps, and blood loss, she was sapped.

The word "Security" was embroidered in white down the guy's black tactical shirtsleeve. His unflinching, steel-gray eyes coldly assessed her. They were the eyes of a man with supreme confidence in his abilities. A mind-read on him yielded only an image of single-minded focus on her. She shivered as a gust of wind pushed at her from behind.

"Who are you, and how do you know Mr. Ryan?" His eyes narrowed.

Kat sighed noisily in frustration. "Ask Matt. We're old friends."

"I need to see some ID."

Kat frowned. ID? *Right.* She must have dropped her purse at Columbia, right before she shifted out and then here. She tapped her feet to wake up her toes. Vertigo swirled in her mind.

Time for mental persuasion ability, again. Twice in one day—far more than she'd attempted in ages. In a low, steady voice she said, "You will let me see Mr. Ryan. You don't need to see my ID. I am who I seem."

Several silent seconds passed during which Kat held her breath. This man had a strong will. Would it work?

An unexpected smile tipped the corners of the muscle man's mouth. "Please, come in. I will arrange for you to see Mr. Ryan."

She suppressed a proud smile as she followed the giant security guard into a sitting room.

"Mr. Ryan is busy at the moment. I'll have Sam check to see when he may be available. Stay here."

"Thanks." She sat heavily on an off-white suede love seat and burrowed deeply into the wool coat, seeking warmth. The pain from her upper arm pulsated. She needed to replace the paper-towel bandage.

Exhaustion drummed through her. Her eyelids drooped as her body slowly warmed.

Her tired brain tried to formulate a plan to deal with Matt. She must ignore her body's reaction and stay in control. Somehow, she must keep him at a distance and convince him to help her. *Absolutely no touching*, she ordered herself. The memory of his kisses blazed through her brain, infusing her body with the kind of heat she hadn't been seeking. Renewed self-disgust surged. What was it about that man?

She snagged a jelly bean out of a glass container on the end table, popped it into her mouth, and relaxed.

Her peripheral vision caught the blurred movement of a four-legged, brown-and-white spotted, furry creature. She smiled when the German shorthaired pointer stuck its nose curiously into the room. In a soothing tone, she said, "I'm just a visitor. No threat."

His head cocked to the side and his ears came up. His tail wagged and he trotted over to her, placing his head in her lap. Animals understood Kat, which was one reason she excelled as a veterinarian, and why she'd gravitated toward the field. She ran her hand lightly along the smooth, shiny coat of his head. "You're in good shape, old man. They must take pretty good care of you."

"This is unexpected," Matt said quietly from the doorway. He granted her his panty-dropping grin.

She immediately straightened from her slouch. Her heart pounded so hard that her ribs ached. The startled dog barked and turned to sit protectively in front of her.

God, Matt was gorgeous. His eyes…his nose—straight, symmetrical, and simply flawless from any angle. And that earring, that hint of the bad boy that made him oh so sexy. *Stop it.*

Her breath hitched when she met the predatory glow in his gaze. She leaned back into the sofa as if that extra few inches of space could protect her from his magnetism. Moments later she felt light-headed and forced herself to slowly release her breath. No matter how badly her body raged with astonishing hormone overload, having a quickie in the Ryan mansion was not on the agenda. Remember, you're injured and you need to talk magical stuff. How exactly did she broach that conversation?

He signaled to the dog, who ignored him. With a smile he muttered, "Insolent mutt." Louder he said, "Come here, Milo." The dog remained in lookout position at Kat's feet. She chewed her lip to suppress a smile at Matt's frustrated frown.

He rolled his eyes. "Milo doesn't like anyone, not even Sam, who feeds him. But he seems to really like you." He whistled commandingly and said, "Here, Milo."

Milo glanced toward Kat, seeking confirmation of the command. She whispered, "Go. I'll be okay." The dog trotted to sit placidly at Matt's left side.

"Traitor," he said as he patted Milo's head. "Are you the dog whisperer or something?"

"I'm pretty good with animals."

"Are you okay? You look…pale."

She met his concerned gaze. "I…it's been a rather eventful day."

"What kind of eventful?"

She sighed. "I don't know why I'm here. Or really how I came to be here. I just am." She expected a what-does-that-mean question to follow.

"Come. Let's go into the office. Take off your coat and I'll order you a drink." Matt turned, plainly expecting her to follow.

Kat's eyes drifted downward as she followed his tall form. His black jeans artfully draped his butt and highlighted his powerful thighs—perfection of shape that just begged to be touched. She cursed herself for noticing. Her face flamed hot.

Entering the office, she kept her eyes purposefully averted, knowing her flushed cheeks gave away too much. The enormous glass windows of the office allowed for an unobstructed one-eighty panorama of the darkening chaos over the bay. "Nice view," she murmured, wandering closer to the window.

"Yes," he said in a tone that suggested his appreciation had nothing to do with the harbor.

As she observed the snow blowing down to the water, she contemplated why something propelled her toward this man. Sure, she wanted him, even though at the moment the pain in her arm overrode that desire. Everything about him was straight out of her most erotic fantasy. She reasoned he couldn't be interested in someone like her beyond the opportunity for another easy lay. She had to focus on her need for his help.

The dull thud of pain in her arm reminded her she needed to take a look at the wound soon. "Would you mind if I used your bathroom?"

He remained silent for a second longer than she expected. She turned her head toward him, raised an eyebrow.

Predatory promise darkened his gaze. A devilish grin lit up his face, sending her into a blushing frenzy.

"End of the hall on the left," he said softly. "Tea, coffee, or something stronger?"

Something stronger sounded good, but an alcohol buzz guaranteed she'd lose control of this situation. "Coffee, please."

Self-conscious, she exited the office, knowing he watched her every step. Milo quickly bounded to her side. Outside the bathroom she smiled at Milo. "You have to wait out here, buddy." He sat down and sent her a pleading look. "I'll just be a moment."

In the bathroom, Kat caught her image in the mirror and cringed. Her face was so pale that the freckles stood out as the only coloration. Her auburn hair had escaped the braid at her back in multiple places, making her look a disheveled mess. She released the braid and shook out her hair, drew it into a ponytail.

She carefully peeled the T-shirt up her arm. Blood had crusted the fabric to her skin in multiple places and still oozed. As a doctor who had stitched up more animal injuries than she could remember, she knew it needed to be flushed and sutured. With no insurance or ID in Otherworld, how was she supposed to get that done? All she could do was hope it wouldn't be long before she shifted back to her life.

Using the sink, she irrigated the wound with lukewarm water. Applying pressure didn't stem the flow of blood. She needed a replacement bandage. Stat.

Before she could search the bathroom for something useful, blackness swarmed the periphery of her vision. Anticipating she was about to shift back to her world, she clawed for the shirt. The last thing she needed was to appear seminaked and bleeding in the middle of some new awkward situation. Her world turned black.

Chapter Ten

Matt glanced impatiently at his desk clock. Kat had been in the bathroom for nearly twenty minutes. Her coffee had come long ago and no longer steamed. No one needed that much time to primp, no matter how nervous she may be. She'd had the wide eyes of a deer in a hunter's crosshairs when she left.

Maybe she jumped to her alternate. He hadn't felt an energy buzz indicative of the power needed for that. Then again, he'd never spent enough time around a Pleiad to know for certain what it felt like when one jumped.

He walked to the bathroom, noting Milo remained camped out vigilantly on the floor in front of the door. He leaned over the dog's body to knock. "Kat, everything okay in there?"

No answer.

Anxiety compressed his chest. *She must've jumped.* "I'm coming in unless you say something." He turned the knob, finding it locked. He glanced down at the dog and nudged him gently with his foot. "Better move, Milo." The dog rose with a grunt and stepped to the side. Using his body strength, he rammed the door until the lock broke.

Kat lay inert on the tile floor. His mind quickly cataloged her partial state of undress and the black lace bra. A bloody bandage lay discarded near the trash can and a scarlet pool had formed on the floor beneath her arm. He lurched to his knees and felt her neck until he found a pulse. He released a pent-up breath of relief.

He shook her, but she didn't stir. To better evaluate the oozing wound on her arm, he gently rolled her. The jagged tear reminded him of similar injuries from his ranger days. Someone shot her? Protective fury flared. Maybe the OLM got to her again, or maybe she'd been shot in her alternate. This woman was amazing. He knew no woman who could tolerate this level of agony without complaining.

Words he hadn't intoned for over a decade fell from Matt's lips in a druid prayer to focus healing power. "*Moí coire coir goiriath, gor rond n-ír. Día dam a dúile dnemrib.*" The healing power within him flowed into her. He allowed her to borrow energy from him.

He halted before he entirely healed the wound on her arm. Her skin was still too pale, but she breathed evenly and her body felt warmer. A final healing session would demonstrate his special ability to her, and perhaps give him an opening to discuss her Pleiades status.

He rolled her onto her back. *What the hell?* Kat had a C-section? The yoga pants were a little too loose, making the area gape open. Did she have a child in her alternate?

A possessive, bitter anger surged. Her giving another man a child was unimaginable. She'd said there wasn't a man waiting for her at home, but maybe there had been. Maybe she'd been married and they divorced. No. No sane heterosexual man would let go of her. She never did answer his question about marriage. Betrayal more vicious than anything he experienced with his dead wife swamped his mind.

One glance at her chest and betrayal and anger drifted away. His heart raced. He stared at the dog tags hanging from her neck.

Holy shit.

He rocked backward and fell onto his butt. He'd thought the OLM had stolen those twin medallions when he, Bryce, and Quinn had been captured while defending a Pleiad who'd thankfully gotten away.

His memories of that week of incarceration remained hazy. The OLM had experimented on him like a lab rat once they discovered his super-healing ability. Then a miraculous woman appeared as if out of thin air and helped him escape. He remembered her voice, but he'd been disoriented from blood loss and the potent drug cocktail the OLM shot into him, not to mention temporarily blinded as a weird drug side effect. He'd assumed the lady was a guilty employee, but hadn't considered Kat.

Memories he'd locked away crowded his brain from a time he'd worked hard to forget.

"Bryce, get Matt out of here. Please. You owe me this." Quinn's eyes drifted closed. When his eyes reopened he stared intently at Bryce. "Come close." Quinn whispered something in Bryce's ear that caused Bryce's gaze to jump to Matt. Loudly Quinn ordered, "Both of you get out of here. Destroy this place. I'm not long for this world."

Bryce backed away from Quinn and grabbed Matt's arm. Matt shrugged him off and yelled. "No! I can help him. We're not leaving him here like this."

Bryce whipped Matt into a headlock. "This is what he wants. I'm sorry for this."

That was the last thing Matt remembered before Bryce knocked him out. He later learned Bryce had carried him from the building. Then he'd blown the place sky high with Quinn inside. The bio-dad he idolized incinerated.

When he regained consciousness, Matt had walked away from Bryce and the druids, recanting any vow he'd ever made to the Society.

Chapter Eleven

Kat clawed her way to consciousness, faintly smelling vanilla potpourri. She scanned the low-lit room—sleek, modern, and in hues of gray. Massive landscape paintings took up most of two walls. She wasn't an art person and couldn't identify the artist, but appreciated their beauty. The room lacked personal items and the random crap that came with being lived in daily. So it must be a guest room.

She pushed to a sit and plucked at an oversize navy-blue T-shirt decorated with a logo she didn't recognize. The shirt was her only clothing other than panties. Where was she? She worried that she'd changed worlds again.

A muscular ache resonated from her right arm. She touched the area. It was bandaged? She peeked beneath the gauze. Her wound had been cleaned and neatly sutured.

A shadow emerged from the corner of the room, moving slowly. "Ready to explain why I found you passed out on my bathroom floor?"

Her gaze jerked to Matt. Relief swept through her that she hadn't done a world jump and ended up in some weirdo's bed. How would he respond to the truth about the wound? She said the first thing that popped into her mind. "You know how to suture?"

"I spent four years as an Army Ranger. I've seen a few bullet wounds." His tone didn't change from its mild timbre. "Who shot you?"

The closer he got, the more vulnerable she felt. His glittering blue eyes never left hers during his slow stalk. Self-preservation had her on hyperalert. She wasn't sure what she feared more: his interrogation mode or the sexual way his gaze slid over her body. She croaked out, "You were a Ranger?"

He halted when only a few feet separated them. His imposing presence sucked the oxygen from the air around her. "What happened?"

Her head buzzed like she'd had a glass or two of wine, which she wanted to blame on his proximity. Most likely exhaustion and blood loss were to blame. A loud stomach growl made her add hunger to the list.

"Why should I trust you?" Her eyes narrowed. "All I really know about you is that you're not loyal to your girlfriends, you treat one-night stands like crap, and apparently you've made quite a name for yourself not only in the business world, but also in the bedroom since we last met."

"Do you even know who's after you?" he demanded. His unblinking gaze intimidated.

She wondered at his tone. He seemed to expect her to answer. Was he trying to use some sort of magic coercion on her? If so, it wasn't working.

He stepped closer. "Did someone else try to kidnap you?" The menace on his face was enough to terrify a normal person into spilling her entire life's story. She suspected he wasn't mad at her, but at her attacker.

She met his determined stare mutely, trying to decipher his mood.

The darkness in his face smoothed into an unreadable intensity. "Please. Tell me what happened this time."

"Another random guy decided to take me out this morning when I refused to be kidnapped. I have no clue why. I don't know who wants to kidnap me or how they found me."

"Damn it. I don't know if I'm angrier that someone shot you, or that you didn't tell me you'd been hurt. What are you into?"

"Nothing." She met his doubtful glower without flinching. "Honestly, I'm not into anything. It's got to be a case of mistaken identity." *Even though the kidnappers knew my name.*

"Are you feeling okay?" he asked gently.

"Yeah. Thanks for fixing me up."

His gaze slid over her face, brow furrowed. "I need you to explain the fact that Katherine Ramsey apparently doesn't exist."

She reeled for a second at the conversation detour. "You had me investigated?"

"What do you expect? You disappeared years ago into thin air. Then you just as suddenly reappeared the other day. So, why don't you exist?"

"That's a bit complicated." She glanced down and fiddled with a loose thread on the comforter.

"Try me. I might understand."

I can travel between worlds. She wanted his help. The words were on the tip of her tongue. But suddenly she still feared he'd judge her crazy. "I'm pretty certain whoever is shooting at me probably isn't interested in you," Of course, that made it sound like she might have a clue why some guys had been after her, which wasn't true.

Matt's lower jaw worked back and forth.

Her heart beat so hard and so fast in response to his intense scrutiny that she felt dizzy and breathless. *You shouldn't be turned on by this.* This now became a more dangerous situation. If he touched her, she was a goner. Then there's being humiliated again. Escape was crucial. She rose from the bed, fully focused on departing.

She announced, "I have to go."

Matt grabbed her arm and halted her. "Sit. We need to talk."

"Let me go." She glared at his hand where it clamped onto her forearm.

In a smooth twist, he lifted her and laid her on the bed, lying on top of her. She wriggled to get away.

"Stop it. You're going to hurt yourself." He gently restrained her beneath him. She bucked against him for freedom. He gripped her wrists and held them above her head, pinning her with the strength of his muscular arms. "Where are you from?" The determined tone was at odds with the concern in his gaze.

"I need to leave." She twisted against him. Thrashing did little to remove his bulk, but it did alert her that he was more than ready to take this to the next level sexually. His ramrod arousal pushed into her thighs.

"Please stop squirming. It's driving me crazy." His tone suggested that irritation had nothing to do with her refusal to answer his questions and everything to do with how much he wanted her.

Her pelvis grazed his cock. He groaned. "Fuck."

She stopped. Her struggle wasn't going to result in freedom, although it did activate every area of skin that contacted his hard body. *Focus, focus, focus. Don't let him get to you.* Somehow she choked out, "Why don't you tell me *what* you are?"

He froze.

They glared at each other in the low light. She wasn't about to divulge more truth. His expression clearly indicated likewise. Stalemate.

"Release me," she requested.

Abruptly, Matt let go of her arms and slid off her. He rested on the edge of the bed and ran a hand through his hair.

Her body screamed denial at the absence of his body's weight. She didn't move even though she'd been freed.

Softly he said, "Ten years ago you started whatever this thing is between us. You cursed me and then disappeared. How do you pop in and out of my life? Are you playing a game?" He massaged his forehead and whispered, "You really are one of the witches, aren't you?"

Witches?

His low, teasing laugh sent a wave of goose bumps down the back of her thighs. Her gaze shot to his. His blue eyes simmered. He had shifted gears. This wasn't the cool, iron will, interrogator Matt. Memory sucked her back to that night so long ago. This was the wild man. The man who exuded passion with each subtle movement. Answering need echoed throughout her body, burning her with the memory of their past.

He leaned over her. His eyes dilated like a cat about to pounce.

"I'm not a witch." She tried to breathe evenly and mask her body's reaction to the idea of being pinned again beneath all those hard contours. So big, broad…and, oh God, she was in trouble. Lust sizzled through her every nerve ending.

He laughed with a deep, rich sound. "Deny it all you want." He lifted her right wrist. His thumb grazed the swirly mark.

A sensual caress shot through her body. She moaned and arched toward him, gasping. "What is that thing?"

He raised his eyebrows and shook his head ever so slightly in what was a look of complete innocence. Or perhaps it was an I'm-not-telling. Then, he shot her a wicked smile before he kissed the mark. His tongue made slow, lazy circles on the inside of her wrist.

It felt as if his tongue trailed a path down her abdomen, although he wasn't touching her anywhere near the path of the intense sensation. The moist roughness paused in the area of her navel. This man was dangerous and not what he seemed. "Stop it," she insisted. She ripped her wrist away from his mouth. "What are you?"

"I may not be so different from you." His gaze dropped to her lips. Subtly, his head dipped.

Oh please, she begged silently. *Do it. Kiss me!*

He wasn't moving fast enough for her. She reached upward, touching her lips to his. Within seconds, he dominated. Covered her again. The thick ridge of his cock pushed tightly against the zipper of his jeans, pressing into her pelvis. His tongue swirled in her mouth. The teasing taste of Scotch saturated her taste buds.

She wanted to control the kiss, and that was what she fought for. But he fought dirty. His might forced her head backward against his powerful biceps as he licked and sucked and drove his tongue against hers until she was trembling.

Then he stopped. And pulled away.

What? Don't stop. Not again.

"Tell me you want this." His eyes were so dilated that the blue was almost lost. He made a slow pelvic circle where their hips were pressed together, then thrust. Her legs drew up around his hips involuntarily as she fought the urge to lock him tight to her.

Pride and the past flickered through her mind. This man made her crazy. She pushed her hands beneath his shirt and knotted her fingers into his chest hair, intending to push him away, but unable. He groaned in a mixture of pain and pleasure. She ran her hands down the corrugated muscles of his abdomen, recognizing the power and reality of the man.

Regular men weren't formed like this. Hollywood actors were either made up to look like this or had implants. And for right now, in this moment, he was all hers.

"I need to know you want this, wildcat. And that you're okay. That your arm doesn't hurt too much. That your head is okay from yesterday." He rained kisses from her ear to her collarbone.

"Yes. I'm fine." She moaned as her eyelids drifted closed. "Please…don't stop."

Their mouths came together hungrily. Her fingers curled deep furrows into the tense muscles of his upper arms. A low groan escaped her.

He broke free of her mouth to yank the T-shirt over her head. A hand covered each breast. He kneaded the tender flesh less than gently and mumbled, "Christ." After a kiss, he swirled his tongue around a nipple.

Her body arched into him.

He halted.

Uncertain why he'd stopped again, she opened her eyes.

He'd pushed up to rest tensely on his forearms. The muscles of his face were pulled tautly over his cheeks as if he was in deep deliberation.

Hadn't they just done this? She couldn't handle his rejection now. She moaned and arched into him.

Hoarsely, he gritted out, "Just tell me this. Are you married?"

"No."

"Is there another man?"

She shook her head, realizing they needed this honesty between them.

His eyes were twin spheres of piercing intensity a moment before he ripped off his own T-shirt. His mouth enveloped one of her spiked nipples. His dark hair fell forward, tickling her skin.

He tore off her panties with vicious impatience. "You're tight. And so wet." His fingers gently massaged her folds, invading and spreading.

Kat undulated her hips, sucking his fingers deep within her. She dug her fingernails into his back. His moan of satisfaction made her grin. Her fingers traced a path to his groin.

"Unzip me," he said against her breast. She carefully pulled at the zipper of his jeans until the ridge of flesh that had been begging for freedom was in her hands. At that moment nothing could've stopped her from palming the fullness. He bowed against her and a low sound rumbled from his chest.

He shimmied out of his pants. In a gravelly voice he warned, "You better hold on. This is going to be a rough ride."

He linked his arm beneath one of her knees and with one powerful drive, he finally plunged into her body driving through the tight, slick folds, lodging so deep.

The pressure was so great that she bit her lip against a scream. She looked up at the undiluted pleasure on his face, but it quickly transformed into a need for more. Her body had little time to adjust before he began to move. Pleasure washed over her at the friction—at that point between pain and pleasure. She threw her head back and scratched long furrows down his arms.

"That's it, wildcat. Give all of yourself to me." He shifted his hand to elevate her pelvis and began a fast tempo. The headboard clanked against the wall with each powerful thrust. She grabbed onto his wrists to lock herself in place.

The powerful strokes coiled her tighter and tighter. The storm spiraling within her was frightening in its strength. Overwhelming. Fear prompted her mind to ask if she trusted him enough for this.

He roughly grated out, "Don't run from me. Not now. This is for both of us." He held her thighs apart to force her to continue to accept the powerful thrusts.

Changing his angle ever so slightly, he hit that one location that turned her world into a starry night. Her body shattered. Muscles rippled, gripped, and clamped down.

At the first rush of her climax, he was right there with her. He came fiercely, filling her and groaning her name as he rolled with her onto his back. He held her tight as the waves continued to burst over them both. His fingers tangled with hers while she buried her face in his neck.

She murmured against his skin, "Please, don't hurt me again."

• • •

Sex had never been this good.

She sprawled against him, naked and weak, with the scent of their combined perspiration. He felt like he'd won the lottery and been two-by-foured at the same time. Everything about this scared the hell out of him. This woman unlike any other had the power to crush him. Irrevocably. And she worried *he'd* hurt *her*?

He wouldn't survive her rejection. He'd spent his youth learning to protect himself against rejection at the hands of the abusive Grant Ryan, who'd hated him for being a bastard son. And a mother who resented that he'd survived birth and was the impetus to turn her husband against her. Then, even though he'd idolized Quinn, his biological father rejected his pleas to remove him from the Ryan household.

The thought of Kat turning to another man like his wife had… He couldn't go there. That was a homicide destined to happen. A fathomless pit of black jealousy gave way to a crushing possessiveness. He needed all men to fear the repercussions of wanting what was his. He'd already marked her, which meant any druid would know to whom she belonged and would keep away.

Yet, it wasn't enough. He needed her. Beyond his terror of her rejection, he wanted to belong to her.

A blast of cold shot down his spine. This went far beyond a paltry curse. This was hard-core bonding shit. The instinct to freak clutched the inside of his skull. He swallowed the urge to jump from the bed and scream denial. He refused to get sucked back into the druid world. He didn't want to do this with a Pleiades. Aw Christ, why did she have to be one of those fucking witches? Why couldn't she just be a run-of-the-mill druidess or even a low-level witch? That he could handle.

And shit, he'd forgotten protection. This was the only woman with whom he lost his mind and had gone without twice. With other women, he religiously protected during sex.

He rolled to his side and released her onto the bed beside him. She was so beautiful. Her auburn lashes fell across her freckled cheek, which now sported a beard burn that he wasn't the least bit guilty about. Hell, beautiful didn't do her justice.

He forced the lust and hunger into a black box in his brain and closed the lid. They needed to do some serious talking. To get her straight on what was going on. Once she accepted the truth that she was a Pleiades, then he'd heal that wound on her arm as proof of his abilities.

He plucked his dog tags off the bedside table. "We need to talk about these."

She rolled toward him, her eyes wide with apprehension. "Who captured you back then?"

"It really was you, wasn't it? I was blinded from some drug the OLM used and weak. They'd done…a lot for many days. I'd just about given up."

She brushed aside the hair on his forehead. "Why did those people do that to you?"

"They hunt people with supernatural abilities to torture and learn about our gifts."

Her eyes widened. She pushed away from him to sit up. "What? You're admitting you have *gifts*? You have supernatural abilities that those wackos would target you for?"

He nodded and bit back a *You do, too*.

"What are your gifts?"

He blew out a rough breath. "Healing myself, and others. I'm not like Wolverine, but I can heal fast."

She ran her hand over the sutured area on her arm. "I did wonder how it healed so fast. I could almost take out the sutures. I might do that at work. Thanks." She cupped his cheek. "It's pretty cool you have that ability. I'm glad I could help you escape. I held onto those tags for you."

He ran his finger over the letters on the tags and gruffly said, "Thanks." Then he draped them back around her neck. "They belong here." His finger trailed down the chain to the cleft between her breasts. "I like the thought of them resting here. How'd you get out of there that day?"

Her gaze darted away from his. "I slipped out."

Damn it. He just revealed one of his biggest secrets. And she wasn't ready to talk about being Pleiades? He blurted out, "You had a C-section?" The minute the question popped out of his mouth he wanted to take it back. How idiotic to release that question unfiltered from his brain to mouth, even if it was his most pressing question. He ran a finger over her scar.

"Yes," she whispered. Her eyes drifted closed.

"When?"

Her eyelids opened, revealing a crushing pain. Tears clung to her eyelashes. "Nine years ago."

"Nine? Were you pregnant when you found me in that OLM facility?"

"I had lost him a few months before."

He couldn't move air through his lungs while his mind did a quick calculation. *Oh God, no.* He dreaded the truth.

But had to know. His throat was so dry he could barely speak. "Was it?"

Tears overflowed her lids. "Yes. He was…yours. I can't take the pill due to some really bad reactions to the medication. Then I met you and protection definitely wasn't on either of our minds that night. A month later I discovered…" Tears slipped down her cheeks. "I didn't quit school, but had to drop out for a semester due to issues with the pregnancy. I went to a shelter for girls for a while since I couldn't live at school. My only family was my aunt, who had pretty much kicked me out of her life at that point. She and I didn't really have a relationship since I was adopted. The woman was a die-hard Christian fundamentalist…the shame of promiscuity and all that jazz."

He pulled her tight to his body. Her tears wet his chest. *Holy hell.* She went through it alone. In a shelter for homeless pregnant women. Impotent fury pressed at him with the need to destroy something. He would've had every resource for her. There wasn't even a question in his mind that he would've done anything. But she wouldn't have needed medicine. He could've fixed whatever was wrong with her and the baby. Quinn could've taught him how. Before he'd died. He wondered why she hadn't considered abortion, even though the thought was abhorrent to him.

As if she'd heard him, she said, "I wanted him so badly. I was mad at you for what happened afterward. And for what you said after we were together. That night seemed magical, and then you pushed me out. But I wanted the baby. He was a gift, but just so weak from the start. Heart defect. He was too little to be born, but my OB didn't think he'd make it to full term. They thought if they brought him out, did heart surgery, and stuck him in one of those incubators for a few months they could save him. Three months early. He was so tiny." She bent her head as her body jerked with sobs. "Twenty-four hours. That was all the life he got."

"Christ, I'm sorry." *A son.* They lost a son. The agony of it burned. He swiped his hand across his moist eyes.

She hugged him tight. "I'm so sorry. I'm sorry for crying all over you. For falling apart after us doing that, which was great. Don't get me wrong. But mostly I'm sorry I lost him. I tried so hard—"

"Don't apologize." He lifted her chin, forcing her to meet his gaze. "It wasn't your fault. Why didn't you shift dimensions and find me?"

"You know about it? About this world-changing thing?"

"A little bit. Why didn't you try to come to me?"

She chewed on her lip. "I didn't know how. I don't have much control over the world changes, even now. They're dimensions? I never thought of that."

He pulled her tight to his body and whispered, "I'm sorry that I couldn't be there to save him."

"I can't have more children. At least my OB recommended not to try again. I had some complications post-op. Almost died."

She almost died. Terror squeezed his gut.

"I named him Matthew," she whispered.

"Oh my God." He groaned and pulled her tighter to him as grief racked her body. His mind splintered into a million shades of shock and pain.

As her tears eased, he asked, "What kind of complications did you have?" She had to be able to have children. She was the flagship of her Pleiad line.

"Uterine infection. Bleeding. My doctor said it wouldn't be advisable to try it again. I probably could, but shouldn't. I might not live through it. As I said before, I don't do well with birth control…so I just avoided until…and we just…oh God." She wiped her tears and suppressed several hiccup sobs.

He didn't miss the implication. She hadn't been with

anyone since the last time they were together. Joy exploded in his chest. She belonged to him. Only him. Dark possession clouded his mind. She would only belong to him. Forever.

Oh hell no. The suffocating terror of entrapment consumed his mind. And gave him focus. They might have good chemistry and he might feel connected to her, but forever? If she was Pleiad, and he was her destined…*oh shit.* This might be the real deal. He wanted to blame their wild chemistry on a curse, but this might be an authentic destined bond. He despised the thought some larger force pushed them together, even if he couldn't imagine being with any other woman. He sure as hell didn't want her seeking out another man.

He said, "We need to talk about what you are. What I am—"

Commotion rose outside the bedroom door. Matt heard a familiar muffled woman's voice. He rolled onto his back and groaned as he threw an arm over his eyes. "You've *got* to be kidding me." *Déjà vu.* Another girlfriend encounter after mind-blowing sex with Kat.

She raised her head from his chest to stare wide-eyed at the door. "It's her, isn't it? Your fiancée. The clothing designer."

Matt gently rolled away from her. "She's not my fiancée. Don't leave. We still need to talk. We have many things to discuss." He fastened his pants and pulled on the discarded T-shirt. He ran a hand through his black hair, ineffectively smoothing its ruffled appearance.

"Is this a habit of yours? Being unfaithful to girlfriends?"

Matt halted with his hand on the door handle. He turned his head to Kat and shot her a crooked half smile. "Only when you decide to *jump* into my world." He pointed at her. "Don't leave."

Matt entered the hall just as Cindy crested the top of the stairs. He closed the door to the bedroom behind him.

Cindy was cleverly dressed, as usual, in colors meant to accent her spray tan and make her baby-blue eyes pop. All that didn't make up for the emaciation she forced on herself, as if she was in competition with the models that displayed her fashions. The bodice of her gown sagged a bit loosely around her chest, suggesting recent weight loss.

She flipped her long hair and marched up to him. After scanning his rumpled disarray, betrayal transformed her face. Her palm connected with his cheek with an echoing crack. "Bastard! Who's in that room?"

"This has nothing to do with you," he said. "Why are you here?" *And how the hell did you get past security and Sam?* he thought.

"I flew back today. Didn't you get the message?"

Matt shook his head and rubbed his cheek. Despite the fact they'd never established their relationship to be monogamous and that he had no plans for matrimony with her, he still felt culpable for hurting her.

"How dare you?" Tears trekked down her cheeks.

"Cindy, we never agreed to be exclusive. I certainly didn't propose."

Her face drained of color. "Everyone warned me about you. They said you'd fuck anything with two legs. That's what caused your first wife to OD."

Matt swallowed his anger. "You should go."

Cindy pushed past him and threw open the bedroom door. Her gaze homed in on Kat. He recognized the sly look on Cindy's face.

Oh shit.

"I just wanted to see who Matt used for the little fling we agreed he needed before we get married. He's already admitted you were nothing more than an itch." She turned and closed the bedroom door behind her.

"Get out."

Cindy smiled and mouthed, "Fuck you." Her spiked heels clicked angrily down the hall away from him.

An energy buzz surrounded his senses. For several seconds he was confused. Then he knew. Kat was leaving. Jumping! His chest squeezed like he was in a pressure tank, and he sucked hard to inflate his lungs. He charged into the bedroom.

Her green eyes narrowed. "I'm leaving before you tell me to this time." Her form flickered.

"No! Goddamn it. Don't you dare shift dimensions before we can talk about what's going on and what you are."

In one blink of his eyes she was gone. He punched the mattress where she'd lain just seconds before.

Chapter Twelve

Damn Matt Ryan. Used by him again. A fling? She thought they had connected. And built upon what they had years ago. That hadn't felt like just another one-time screw. She thought she read genuine sadness from him about the baby. What an idealistic idiot she was.

How could he possibly consider marrying that Cindy woman? No one with any proprietary thoughts about him would allow another woman to touch him, let alone have a sanctified fling. Images of Matt with Cindy tortured her brain. She forced herself to breathe slowly and beat back the pain in her chest.

The coldly rational side of her mind pointed out that she could be pregnant again. By him. She wouldn't survive it, and not just from a medical perspective. It would kill her this time, if she lost another child. Panic hit. Her chest clinched tight until she could barely breathe.

Don't think about it, she ordered herself. *Chances are low. Timing is wrong.*

She focused on thinking of nothing. Meditating on clean,

pure nothing.

But his final words replayed in her head over and over: *Don't you dare shift dimensions before we can talk about what's going on and what you are.*

He knew she was a jumper and called her a witch. A witch? She couldn't do fictional witchy things, although it might be cool to start a candle with a finger snap or stir her cup from a distance. Maybe she could do those things. She'd just never tried. Regardless, she wondered how long he'd known what she was.

A loud knock resonated through her apartment from the front door.

Kat dragged herself upright, grabbed her robe from the bathroom, and headed toward the front door. Peeping through the door's privacy hole, she saw Riley. She leaned her head against the door and groaned. It wasn't a.m.; it was p.m. He wanted to drag her to that Wiccan thing.

His muffled voice filtered through the door. "I can hear you. Open up."

She unlatched the chain, threw the dead bolt, and opened the door wide.

Riley gave her a good once-over. "Well, don't you just look like shit. Is that beard burn on your cheek?"

"Shut up."

"It happened again, didn't it? You disappeared." He gave her a thorough once-over with a knowing leer. "And got busy."

Her cheeks flamed. "I'm not really up to attending a Wiccan thing tonight."

Riley pushed through the door into her apartment. "Listen, girlie-girl, I covered for you at work today. You owe me. Just remember you were visiting your sick aunt in Wilmington. Of course, our boss thinks you're interviewing for a new job down there." Riley headed for the kitchen and helped himself to bottled water from her fridge. After a big slog, he leaned against the counter and smiled. "On a scale of one to ten, how hot was he?"

She scowled.

"One to ten?" he prompted while waving the bottle in her direction.

"Twenty." A small smile broke on her face. "I'm taking a shower."

Riley laughed. "Just be sure to put on something other than that ratty robe. Jesus, when did you buy that thing? Last century? We need to go shopping and get you some sexy clothes. Make it a speedy shower. We are going to the meeting."

"I'm too tired," she yelled from the bathroom.

"I don't care if you had three days of gymnastics with Mr. Twenty. You've got a problem. This woman might have answers."

She stepped into the shower and sighed as the warm water soothed her skin. As much as she hated to admit it, Riley might be right. She needed answers.

• • •

A discordant chime rang out.

Riley led Kat to a space on the floor. "Take a seat. We all sit in as much of a circle as possible. Our High Priestess, Amy, will likely start us out."

A short redhead with wildly askew brown hair wearing Birkenstocks and a billowing black skirt made some broad motions with her arm spreading the smoke from incense around her body. "Welcome brothers and sisters. Today I am so pleased to introduce Charlotte Stratford, who visits us again from…" Amy glanced sidelong at the blonde sitting next to her, who had to be well into her late forties.

"Alabama," Charlotte said in a deep Southern drawl.

She pushed at her blond hair, which was pulled into a loose, chaotic bun. Little could be discerned of her body beneath a teal, gauzy dress. As she shifted, the multitude of crystals around her neck tinkled softly.

"Right. She's going to speak to us about time travel," resumed Amy.

Time travel? Kat was suddenly very interested in this speaker.

"Thanks, y'all, for inviting me into your midst today. I'm not going to speak about time travel." Charlotte rolled her gray eyes. "Come on. That's ridiculous. Instead, I'd like to discuss the Pleiades, the women of Greek mythology who supposedly form this constellation."

Kat sat up straight, goose bumps popping out on her arms.

"They were seven sisters. The myths written of the Pleiades sisters are confusing and often contradictory, but intriguing. The myth recounts that after seven years of being pursued by Orion, the sisters were each given the option to escape to an alternate dimension and avoid Orion's advances, if she wanted. That which we see twinkling in the sky is but a reflection of the path she travels from one aspect of the universe to another."

Charlotte paused and made eye contact with Kat. She said slowly, "From one dimension of this world to another." A disturbing glint of knowledge shone in her pale, perceptive gaze when it locked onto hers. Charlotte's gaze drifted to Kat's wrist.

She pulled her shirtsleeve over the mark.

The older woman's mouth curved into a small smile.

Kat's spine went rigid, warning chills racing down her back. This woman knew about her. And that freaked her out.

Charlotte smiled. "The sisters are the keepers of the veil. This is where Greek myth meets Celtic Druidic legend. It is said the Pleiades must convene on the last night of Samhain, that's November second, every twenty years to assure the ancestors all is well in our world. If not, the ancestors will cross in anger. Then chaos will ensue. And that means Armageddon."

Amy interrupted with a know-it-all tone. "That makes no sense. Druids revere the spirits of the departed. They think of them as sources of guidance and inspiration. Not as evil."

Charlotte nodded. "Absolutely. On this day of Samhain, it is essential that the Pleiades commune with their descendants. If not, they risk inciting the wrath of gods. And then the veil will fall, allowing those ancestors to cross."

Someone asked, "Aren't the Pleiades immortal goddesses? If so, I don't understand how they'd have dead descendants."

Charlotte shifted her legs. "Well…we've all heard of the promiscuity of the Greek deities, have we not? These women are their human descendants. The first daughter in each line inherits the Pleiades' gifts."

Memories that didn't make sense skittered through Kat's brain. Charlotte's Greek myth was a childhood tale she'd heard before. Many times. Only never from the family she grew up with in South Carolina. Instead, she envisioned a pretty redhead. The myth she'd been told claimed the descendant women were human and they could travel between dimensions, but Kat recalled more details than Charlotte had revealed. Details about the sisters. There were seven, each gifted with unique abilities that were passed to the first daughter in each line. Their protectors were the Sentry druids, who not only revered them, but also amongst that warrior elite lay a destined match for each of those seven women, a love that couldn't be denied.

Her mind skittered to Matt.

Her storyteller of memory had been one of those women. A beautiful strawberry-blonde Pleiad with freckles across her nose and cheeks. A woman she had called…

Mommy.

Chills exploded down her arms. A confusing vision materialized in her mind. A memory?

"Why are we here, Mommy?" Kat squinted against the pain of the light hitting her eyes. She clung tightly to her mother's neck. The smell of salty air close to an ocean hit her sensitive nose, and the sound of waves echoed in her ears.

"Katie-kat, you've got to let go."

"No, Mommy. I want to go back to the zoo. You promised we'd see the giraffes today. You want to leave me here. I can read your thoughts. I know it's true 'cause you're crying."

"Those bad men shot me with a dart full of medicine that's going to make me die unless they give me the antidote. My only chance to see you again is to go back. To get the good drug that will cure me. These bad men don't know about you. They must never find out about you. They don't care that you're only ten. They'll hurt you. I need you to stay here until I can come get you."

"You're going to die? I'm scared, Mommy." Kat fought as her mother pried her arms from around her neck. "I love you, Mommy. Mommy! Don't leave me."

"You've got to be Mommy's brave girl now, sweetheart. I love you. And I need you to survive." She gave Kat a hug and kissed her. "Someday you may understand. Your father may never forgive me for this. I'm sorry."

Kat pressed on her eyeballs to ease the pounding head pain. When that failed, she massaged each eye socket, an acupuncture move a colleague mentioned years ago. It'd worked before for mini-migraines. Abruptly, the pain cleared. Hallelujah. Was that a memory or a movie scene? Seemed so real. Grief clouded her mind. Grief over what? Loss of that woman in the weird vision?

She couldn't recall anything about the woman other than that fleeting memory. She pushed her brain to remember something else. Anything that might explain what was happening to her. Pressing her mind for more info was like flailing against a wall.

Nothing.

Her reward was a throbbing headache so brutal that her stomach knotted. She whispered to Riley, "I've got to go. Must've been something in the cake, but I feel like I'm going to puke."

Kat got up and walked briskly toward the front door. She hadn't realized how stifled she'd felt until she was outside in the crisp evening air. She closed her eyes and focused on the image of the strawberry-blonde woman with the long hair.

A new memory surfaced. It was associated with intense embarrassment. She had dropped a pan of brownie dough on the kitchen floor before it made it to the oven. Brownies she needed for her class Christmas party. Comforting laughter surrounded her seconds before long blonde hair and warmth enclosed her in a hug.

Her life here in this dimension was a sham. Who was she? And where was her mother? And her real father. Of him, she recalled nothing.

Chapter Thirteen

Matt's secretary greeted him as he exited the elevator on the fifteenth floor. She pursed her lips, disapproval in her narrowed gaze. "You're late."

Matt shrugged. He should take issue with her attitude, but he was too frustrated and too tired.

She followed him into his office. "There's someone here to see you. He's been waiting about thirty minutes. You must meet with him. This is not a person that takes no for an answer."

"What happened to scheduling an appointment?" Matt muttered as he sifted through the mail on his desk. He caught the aggravated glower she cast his way. "Who is it?"

"Bryce Sinclair. He is…very persuasive."

"Where is he?" he snapped, infuriated that Bryce cornered him into a meeting.

"Conference room on the tenth floor."

"Fine. I'll head down there." He stormed back toward the elevator.

He entered the conference room with the taste of

irritation in back of his throat. He'd recognized the energy buzz the second he got off the elevator. Druids. As in plural, which meant the old bastard had brought back up. This guaranteed to be on its way to nowhere good.

The chair at the far end of the table was toward the window. To the right sat a college-age boy whose chiseled features could've been straight from a page in *GQ*. The kid's stylized brown hair was sculpted into trendy spikes. His gaze darted to Matt, curious and nonjudgmental. A low-grade energy buzz identified him as a young Sentry.

The head chair rotated with a soft hiss. And Matt's irritation jumped straight to need-to-pulverize. He struggled to project only indifference, but he couldn't help the bitterness in his tone. "Bryce. I'd say it was a pleasure to see you, but I'd be lying. Who's your friend?"

"You look tired, Matt. Trouble sleeping?" Bryce raised his eyebrows.

Matt sauntered to the bar and poured himself a glass of Perrier. "Can I get either of you a drink?"

"No thanks," said the spiky-haired guy.

Bryce shook his head.

Between silent sips of Perrier, he evaluated Bryce suspiciously.

Bryce waved at the guy next to him. "This is Jason." Bryce scanned Matt in a silent, critical once-over and then ordered, "Take a seat. We are going to have that little chat you've been avoiding."

"Why are you here?" Matt shot Bryce an unflinching glare as he took a seat. His scrutiny transferred to Jason.

To the kid's credit, Jason held eye contact, but his gaze lacked the fuck-you inherent to all trained and tested Sentry. He couldn't be Bryce's bodyguard—a little too green behind the gills.

"What would you like to talk about? But let me add that

I still couldn't care less about druid problems."

"Strange. Wasn't it you who rescued Katherine the other night? And healed her? I can't tell you how much we appreciated that. She is, as you well know, important."

Matt crunched his molars together and swore he would kill Eli. "Coincidence. I was in the right place at the right time. Nothing more."

"Where is she?"

"I don't know. She could be in the city or back in her dimension. I know you don't need me as a tracker here in the city. You've got people far better than me."

"You're good, but I've got others for that. I want to actually talk about Katherine Ramsey. You're the only person to have spent some time with her."

Matt swallowed his impulse to insist Bryce stay away from her. She needed Bryce's protective circle whenever she decided to jump back to this dimension. If only his gut didn't prompt him to do anything other than what Bryce wanted. "How about you tell me what you already know."

"She has appeared suddenly in this dimension. Her relative lack of background and the detection of some sort of power in her suggests to me she's my missing Pleiad. Eli indicated the two of you might've met before. We feel Jason might be her destined, which is why he's here today."

Not fucking likely. Possessive fury lit his brain.

"How do you know Katherine?"

"We met several years ago." Matt visibly relaxed. That little prick had never met Kat. She didn't go by her full name.

"When?"

"How do *you* know her, Jason?" Matt countered.

Jason opened his mouth to speak, but Bryce rested a hand on his arm. "He's baiting you."

If that kid touched her, Matt swore he'd kill the wuss without remorse. He would make sure his death was painful and ugly. *Shit.* This must be part of bonding to a Pleiad. Hell, he was already committed to defending his turf. *No, no, no!* There was no way some universal force beyond his control was meddling with his life to get him on bended knee with a goddamned ring.

Bryce asked, "Where is she now?"

"I suspect she's back in her other dimension."

"Oh." Bryce sighed.

The sadness bordering on grief overshadowing Bryce's face surprised Matt. Bryce had never struck him as one to be sentimental where the Pleiades were concerned. Protective and dictatorial, sure—that was his job. Attached, no.

Bryce cleared his throat before asking hoarsely, "When do you expect her back?

"I don't know. She doesn't seem to have control over her power. It's not like she gave me her itinerary before she popped away."

Bryce leaned forward. "She is our seventh, isn't she?"

"It's likely, but we didn't exactly clarify that."

Bryce crossed his arms. "What exactly did you talk about, then? Eli said you spoke with her."

Matt resented Bryce's tone that suggested he was an adolescent one screwup away from being grounded. Matt said, "Being Pleiad isn't exactly a simple subject to broach, especially since she doesn't seem to know anything. Now, why is that, Bryce? Why is a Pleiades lost in her alternate and doesn't know what she really is?"

Bryce remained silent.

Matt continued, "Besides, why didn't she gravitate toward lover boy over there when she's in this dimension? Aren't destineds usually attracted through some sort of greater force or something?"

Bryce cocked an eyebrow questioningly at Jason.

"I don't know. I thought I brought this up to you already.

I mean, I *think* we're supposed to be together."

Something was going on and Matt didn't like not having full intel. Who the hell was Jason, and why hadn't he met her if he was claiming to be her destined?

"You should've called me, Matt, when you were suspicious she was the one I sought," Bryce said.

"Your lost girls aren't my problem. Why isn't she here in the Sourceworld full time to begin with?"

Bryce hesitated and blew out a long breath. "Her mother jumped her away at a young age to protect her. Katherine comes from the mind-bender line. Seems that her mother mind-wiped her before depositing her in the other dimension. That was right before the OLM killed her mother. We need Katherine here to complete the heptagon. If she comes back to you again, I want you to bring her to us. We need to prepare her for the Confirmation this weekend."

Mind-wiped? Kat really had no clue what was going on. How he wished he could take back how he handled yesterday and perhaps be gentler in his questioning. He crossed his arms in front of his chest. "I don't do favors for you anymore. Not my problem. Besides, if Jason is her destined, then he should be her focal point to entering this dimension. Not me. So your problem is solved. This meeting is over. I'm sure you two can find your own way out." He rose and headed for the door.

He pulled it open, but it pulled away from him, slammed shut, and locked. "Bryce, I'm in no mood for games. We're done here." A tickle of fear entered his mind. Bryce's mental power was unique, and lethal, when he chose to use it.

Bryce rose. "You and I are not done."

He turned and narrowed his eyes. He thought, *Bring it on, old man*, even though he was pretty certain Bryce couldn't read thoughts—just telekinesis and the mind crunch. Fuck, he hoped the old bastard didn't resort to that.

Bryce turned to Jason. "Leave us."

"But you said—"

Bryce turned the full force of his anger on the kid. "Get. The. Fuck. Out."

Jason scurried around Matt. The door unlocked for him.

The energy in the room sizzled. Matt's head buzzed.

Bryce was revved up. "You are going to hear me out. I don't know why the gods chose you to be her focal point. Frankly, I don't give a flying fuck. You will do whatever you need to in order to get her to me. If you have to charm her, then—"Bryce sucked in a deep breath and whooshed out, "Do it. You are not allowed to sleep with her. There is no long-term for you and her. As a deserter, you aren't worthy of her. She's got her destined arranged. All I care about is that you ground her here and bring her to me. Don't hide her. Don't take her to bed. Bring her to me."

"Go to hell." Spikes of white-hot fury lacerated his mind. Bryce considered him as unscrupulous as Grant Ryan, who'd regularly crossed that ethical line to accomplish anything that needed to be done. Sex, threats, murder, blackmail…none of it mattered to Grant, just as long as he got what he wanted.

Matt had never crossed that line. And he sure as hell wouldn't now.

"If you don't, I've prepared a full disclosure packet and will present it to your sister. How do you think that frail thing would react to knowing about Quinn? To discover Grant wasn't your father? That you're a druid bastard?" He clucked.

Matt backed against the door, aghast. Was he bluffing? Bryce revered women, protected them. He whispered, "You wouldn't."

"You've put me in a tight spot, Matt. I'd do just about anything to get her back at this point. To get her to safety. We're coming down to the wire on the Confirmation. The OLM has teams hunting for her. It's my job to protect this world, and her."

Matt exploded across the room, going for Bryce's jugular. "Stay away from Allison." Bryce didn't move. Before he could get closer than a few inches from Bryce's body, he was thrown backward by an invisible force. He crashed into the wall. A crushing pain consumed his brain. He slithered to the floor, clutching his skull. The overwhelming pain stopped.

Bryce hovered above him. "If you don't get her to me when she reappears, the packet goes out. Do we have an understanding?"

Matt remained silent.

The pain inside his skull resumed. He moaned. Reluctantly, he gritted out, "Yes."

Chapter Fourteen

Matt slid into the booth at the Long Beach diner. He massaged his head, which still throbbed from his encounter with Bryce.

Eli grinned. "You look like crap." Eli's worn ball cap, wrinkled button-down shirt, and jeans suggested many days of wear. His new laissez-faire attitude on life grated on Matt. But ever since Eli quit MI6, his care for the little things had become nonexistent.

"Did you find out where Kat went when she left my office? Anything about where she's from?"

"That recording of her…" Eli whistled low and did a hand outline of an hourglass silhouette, rewinding over the chest part.

"You are headed for a bloody nose."

Eli shook his head. "You got it bad, bro. Bad. She must be good, especially in hallways."

"Asshole. You weren't supposed to watch the whole recording."

"Did she start it or did you or was it kind of a dual attack? I had a tough time telling. But…kind of disappointing that you pulled back."

His neck heated. "Did you even shower today?"

"Interesting deflection." Eli shrugged. "Can't remember."

"What is going on with you? You've spent more nights at my place in the past month than yours. You drink until you pass out…"

"Chasing demons." Eli adjusted his baseball cap and wouldn't meet Matt's gaze.

"All right, fine, don't tell me. I just want to know if you completed Kat's background."

Eli grabbed a laminated menu from behind the napkin dispenser. "I wonder if they serve breakfast twenty-four-seven. I could really go for some waffles."

"It's dinner time. You can ask." Matt scowled. "Background…"

"Sure. It's done. It's thin, but for most cursory glances it'll hold. The only image I could isolate off the video that didn't have you in it was an awful picture." Eli stared intently at Matt for a few seconds, and then his laughter rippled through the air. His white teeth presented a startling contrast to his tanned skin and ear-length, dark hair.

"Now what's funny?" Matt asked, only briefly glancing up from the menu.

"She left your ass. There's no other reason for you to be so bloody peevish. Was it before or after you and she…? You two were headed for it based on the security footage."

Matt's jaw tightened. "I'll knock out those expensive teeth you just had fixed if you don't lay off this right now."

"You are so fucked." Eli went back to chuckling to himself as he looked at the menu.

"What exactly is that supposed to mean?"

"Fate's a fickle bitch, Matt. I've warned you that one day she was going to creep up and bite you in the ass. You live in denial. Eventually, you'll come to terms with the fact that you are one of us. And, apparently one with a big destiny." A slow smile spread across his face.

"You sound like Yoda." The coolness of Matt's tone suggested he wasn't amused.

"The truth me see." Eli tented his hands in front of his face. "I just can't believe that you'd get chosen for one of those girls."

"I am *not* her destined."

"Really? She's popping in and out of your life. You practically boffed her in a hallway. If you're not destined, then how would you feel about someone else, a different druid, with his hands on her? Licking her?"

His mind hazed red. He shot over the table and jabbed Eli in the throat. Not enough to kill him, but a warning. "Stop this right now."

Eli coughed and grabbed for his tea. "I might've deserved that, but that woman is driving you nuts. And I'm right."

He glared at Eli, hating how well his brother knew him. His level of freak-out over Kat and potential bonding only fueled his short fuse.

Eli shrugged off the attack. "How's she doing after Acquisitions went after her?"

Matt gave the waitress his order. Then resumed, "You're not the first person today to ask me about her."

Eli frowned and cursed under his breath. "What did Bryce do to you?"

Matt massaged his temple, somehow comforted that if he ever faced off against Bryce, his brother would be on his team.

"He didn't," Eli said. "A mind crunch? What else?"

"Threatened me with Allison. To reveal you and Quinn."

"That's…not Bryce. He's about protection, not threats. This situation must be driving him to the edge. You know we need her, well all seven of the girls to be in attendance… Cripes, it's in two days or something, I think." Eli took a sip of ice tea.

"What I can't figure out is his angle with that Jason kid." He gritted his teeth against renewed violence when he imagined Jason touching her.

"The one Bryce claims is matched with Kat?"

He nodded.

Eli smiled. "Uh, right. Whatever on that one. I know his family. They're a good bunch. Excellent druid powers in that line, but I think it must skip a generation because Jason is kind of a dud. He's got some mediocre precog skills, but that's about it. He's in training for Sentry, but I'm not sure he'll make it. I think Bryce wants them to be matched because he can intimidate the kid into doing what he wants. What I don't understand is why Bryce doesn't get that he can't play God. Just because you go along with some bullshit this kid claims he saw in a random dream, and you want it to happen, doesn't mean it's going to work."

"What exactly are Kat's supposed powers?" asked Matt.

"You don't know?" A slow grin spread on Eli's face. "That's rich."

"Bryce mentioned mind-bending. What exactly does that mean?"

"Not that Bryce has publicly divulged this, but as a mind-bender she should be able to read minds, change minds, coerce. That type of stuff. She try anything on you?"

"No." At least not that he was aware of.

"You probably wouldn't know if she did her magic on you. But since you and she are probably you know what to each other, that means she *might* not be able to use her stuff on you."

"We are not…" he paused and gritted out, "destined." His tone suggested that pushing this topic would result in more pain.

Eli raised his tea glass in silent acquiescence and took a

sip.

Matt observed two men enter the diner. In a quiet voice he said, "Two guys just came in and scanned this place. Trained operatives. Maybe Acquisitions. They're at your back in the booth close to the front door."

Eli stood and sauntered in the direction of their waitress who was at a table close to the entrance. He slid into a gentile Southern accent. "Ma'am, hate to bother, but could I get a refill on the tea." He smiled charmingly through her bubbly consent, then returned to the table.

Eli leaned back in the booth and threw his arms wide. To the world he appeared to be enjoying himself immensely. He slid back to his British accent. "OLM. No doubt. They're carrying and I saw a zip tie hanging out of a pocket. Probably Acquisition shites. There are two more of them outside in the navy SUV. What protection you packing?"

"One piece. You?"

"Ankle, but it's more of a toy. If we can get to my truck, then we're good. Suggestions?"

"They won't take us in here. Too many witnesses. We need to get out before they snap photos. I do not want to be on the OLM's bulletin board of Most Wanted Weirdoes."

"The real question is what they're doing here. Do they seem to you like we're their targets?" Eli swirled the ice in his tea.

He watched the men covertly for a minute. "No."

Bryce's supposition that he was Kat's focal point to enter this dimension slid through his mind. In this one instance, he hoped she wouldn't come to him. Not here and definitely not now.

• • •

Nine twenty-five p.m. according to the stove clock. Kat kicked off her shoes next to the kitchen counter and slid her keys onto the slick surface with a bit too much momentum. They slid off the other side and clattered on the floor. *Great.* Perfect ending for a too-long day.

Her head still howled in complaint over the memory bursts from earlier, and the argument she'd had with Riley to ensure him that she'd be fine if he dropped her off.

Her stomach growled, and she stood at the open freezer contemplating the slim selection of microwave dinners and four wild-berry popsicles. She read the nutritional information on a chicken concoction that would probably taste like salty garlic and slid it back into the freezer. She snagged an apple and pulled out the cutting board. Three slices and the knife slipped, its point slicing her wrist. The laceration had penetrated the tip of Matt's swirly triangle mark. Damn it.

She pressed a towel over the laceration and wished for Matt. Maybe he could fix this. The last thing she wanted was an ER visit right now. Her thumb rubbed over the mark to the point it created a heated friction in addition to bleeding. She thought desperately, *Get me out of here. Take me to him.*

The world spun.

• • •

Matt sipped coffee. His taste buds cringed and he resisted the urge to spit the swill back into the cup. His phone vibrated across the table. Without checking the number he answered gruffly, "What?"

"Matthew, she needs you. She's coming back. It's up to you, now," said a young woman.

"Nicole?" Alarm vise-gripped his gut. Maybe the nineteen year-old Pleiad precog had a vision.

"Ground her to this world. Protect her and bring her to us. Don't let them get her. She won't trust anyone else."

Matt gripped the phone tighter. “Your voice sounds funny.”

Silence came from the other end.

“You still there, Nicole?” Matt pressed the phone to his ear, detecting breathing.

She asked in a small voice, “Who am I on the phone with?”

“Matt Ryan.”

“Why are we on the phone?”

“You tell me. We haven’t spoken since I left the Society. I think you had one of your episodes. Can you remember?”

“How did I even know your number? This precog thing is embarrassing. What did I say?”

“I think you suspect the missing Pleiad is about to be found.”

“Really? Then why would I call you and not Bryce? I’m sorry I bothered you. We miss you. You must come visit.”

“Bye, Nicole.”

The mark on his wrist burned a few seconds after he disconnected the call. A sharp sting evocative of a knife blade penetrated the area. “We’ve got to leave. Now. There’s about to be a situation.”

Eli set down his ice tea and tensed. “Was that our Nicole on the phone?”

“She had a vision. Something’s about to happen.”

“What’s the plan?”

“Your truck. You’re going to lose the Acquisitions guys while I take care of our extra passenger.”

“What extra passenger? What about that POS you drove down here.” Eli squinted through the window.

Matt threw two twenties on the table and headed for the exit with Eli on his hells. “Forget the car. We need to stick together.” The buzz of psychic energy surrounded him. “You feel it? She’s coming.”

Kat's form materialized ten feet in front of him on the asphalt as they exited the diner. His mind froze at the sight of the blood-soaked towel she pressed to her wrist. Had she tried to suicide herself? Holy shit.

Disoriented green eyes scanned the area. Her lower lip trembled. She squinted at him as if she couldn't quite make him out.

He swallowed hard in an attempt to put a lid on the fear powering through him. With a bit more force than necessary he asked, "What happened?"

"Matt?" she croaked out in a barely discernible whisper. "God, my eyes hurt. I had a bit of an accident."

Relief that she hadn't been suiciding herself calmed his mind. "You picked a really shitty time to pop in." He eyed the Acquisitions Team. They were on the move with weapons in full view. He scooped her off the ground and sprinted toward Eli's double-cab truck. A bullet pierced the side of the truck just as he slammed the door. A second one grazed his shoulder as it pierced the truck's metal.

Eli squealed the tires on his rush out of the lot. "Hang on. They're following. Goddamned Sighter must've predicted this."

"What the hell!" he bellowed as he shot off the seat with Kat in his lap. "I just got ass-fucked by an orange soda can. Did a garbage bag explode back here or something, Eli?" He threw the offending can at the dashboard.

"Watch it!" Eli yelled as he ducked the ricocheting can.

The car swerved, throwing them tight against the passenger side of the rear seat.

"Who's chasing us?" she asked.

"OLM." He held her tight in his arms. They slammed from one end of the seat to the other with each sharp turn, garbage piercing through his clothes. "Why are you bleeding? What happened?"

Eli glanced at them through the rearview mirror. “She’s making a bloody mess all over my seat. Can you put a stop to that?”

“Like you’d notice with all the trash back here. You drive and I’ll take care of her.”

He peeled her away from him. “What happened?” He unwrapped the towel while keeping her steady between his thighs.

“I cut myself trying to slice an apple. Stupid, really. Is that guy chasing us associated with the same guy who attacked me the other night?”

“Yes. The OLM.” He hissed when he saw the deep laceration. “You did a number on yourself.”

She nodded.

“Wildcat, I need for you to trust me. I’m going to help you. Okay?”

“Hospital?”

“No time.” He allowed a small amount of the Voice to infuse his tone. “You’re going to let me help you.”

She nodded mutely and gave him a brave smile. She whispered, “That’s why I came to you.”

The confidence and trust shining in her eyes gut-punched him. That look had nothing to do with his use of the Voice.

His eyes met Eli’s concerned gaze in the rearview mirror for a split second. He was terrified for his own hide during the time Matt unleashed his ability. “I got it, Eli. You can keep driving. I won’t steal energy from you.”

Eli nodded. The worry smoothed into concentration.

Healing power heated his palms while he concentrated on her laceration. He ran a hand over the cut until only a pink pucker of scarring remained. Her eyelids drooped in drowsiness, a common side effect after a healing session. He held her tightly as the truck careered around a curve.

“Matt, I need you to take out the bastard behind us. These

stoplights are a nightmare for ditching them," Eli said.

"A gunfight on highway twenty-seven isn't what I'd call keeping it low-key."

"Fuck low-key. They're the ones shooting at us."

Eli squealed the tire wheels on a sharp right. "Okay. I'll try to get off the highway."

"Just get away from them." He opened the side window and leaned out, aiming his Glock at the dark Suburban kissing their bumper. Before he could fire, the truck shuddered and then madly swerved. "What the…?" He was thrown hard against the half-open window.

Eli fought with the steering wheel. "They must've shot a tire. Bloody hell, hang on!"

The truck caught the curb and entered a roll. Matt clutched Kat against him protectively as they were thrown around the backseat. His head took a numbing blow against the door. He heard her scream. *I can't pass out.* Darkness clouded his mind.

Chapter Fifteen

The truck came to rest passenger side down near a stone wall. Kat worked her jaw free of its clench. A quick exam found she had a few scrapes, but no life-threatening injury. Matt had taken most of the hits as they rolled, keeping her pulled into his body. Rotating her previously lacerated forearm into view showed all that remained of the damage was a small pink line of scarring. Wow.

She shifted off him, trying to balance her weight against the back of the front seat, which was difficult given the odd angle and limited space. This man really wasn't what he seemed. What he was…well, she still wasn't entirely clear on that. The Pleiades myth ran through her mind, making her wonder if he was druid.

She shook him with one hand while balancing with the other. "Matt?"

He didn't respond. A brutal shard of glass protruded from his left arm. There was a lot of blood. She assessed the amount of blood lost based on a pile of the congealing mess. That level of uncontrolled hemorrhage was not compatible with life.

She glanced into the front seat and caught Eli's troubled stare from his position dangling in the seat belt. He had a gash on his head that gushed blood. After a momentary what-the-hell she blurted, "You're Matt's brother?"

"Yep."

"Matt looks pretty bad," Kat said, glancing down again.

"He's more than pretty bad. He's checking out. He gave you way too much energy when he healed you and hasn't got anything left for himself."

"What?"

Eli cut himself out of the seat belt. With a grunt, he landed against the passenger door.

He reached over the seat. "Fuck. He's too damaged for me to help him. I've got a bit of healing ability like him, but it's not strong enough. Listen, little Pleiad, it's time for you to do your stuff on him. Before he's gone. And before we have company." Eli pulled himself to the edge of the car to see out the driver's window. "Acquisitions is probably on its way and I'm sure there's a nosy Good Samaritan around here."

"What did you call me?"

"Cripes. Don't you know anything?"

"What do you think I am?"

"You're one of the Pleiades."

Kat shot him a get-real glare.

"Okay, let me give you the footnotes version. You are one of the seven Pleiades. They're like—"

"I know about the sisters, but that's just a weird Greek myth," she interrupted.

"Then you're in the dead center of one of the wackiest of the Greek myths imaginable. You are a direct descendant of one of the seven."

"I'm not a Pleiades Goddess."

Eli massaged his forehead where a large purpling bump had appeared. "'Course you're not a goddess. But you are descended from one. Don't give me that you're-a-nutter look again. You just materialized in front of us. Definitely a Pleiad trick. Listen, amnesia and identity crisis aside, what matters right now is that you are Pleiades. Each one of you lucky ladies is destined to bond to a druid. Some god oversees which unlucky bastard has to serve as sperm donor to the next generation. This God must've matched you to Matt. Too bad it wasn't me. I'd happily worship that beautiful little body of yours and introduce you to the eccentricities of the Druides Society." He smiled and scanned her chest. "Unfortunately, you got Matt who has major issues about involvement in anything that has to do with Pleiades or druids, not to mention women and permanent attachment. Those unfortunate problems are for the two of you to work out on your own time."

Kat stared at Matt, terrified he'd die.

Eli pulled himself to the driver-side window again to glance outside and then eased back into the car. "The really bad news is he can die and is right now on the express bus to the afterlife. The irony is if he dies, then so does your line. That's the Pleiades line. That really isn't an option. Because the gods know this fact, they designed the bonding thing to work so that each partner has the capability to give back what the other needs to pull him back from death. Some genetic code in you knows what to do."

"What do I do?" She ran her hands over Matt's chest, unable to detect a heartbeat. She felt his neck and detected weak pulsation.

Eli shrugged in reply. "Don't know. But I'd prefer my brother not die. So, get on with it."

Panic set in when she no longer felt a pulse beneath her fingers. "Call nine-one-one!"

"He'll die before they arrive. Hell, the Acquisitions team on its way will kill us all long before they get here." Eli didn't move, but continued to watch her expectantly.

"What do you think I'm supposed to do?"

Eli raised his eyebrows in a clear *I-don't-know*.

"How does Matt's healing thing work?" Kat probed a finger gently around the large glass shard.

"Requires he take energy to give back energy."

"So, where do you think he got the energy to give to me?"

"Looks like himself since I'm feeling fine. He usually doesn't do that."

"What does that mean?" Kat frowned.

"He borrows energy from other living people or animals around him. He must like you a bit more than he's willing to admit, even to himself." Eli chuckled

Why was the bastard laughing?

"I think it's time for you to do your magic, little Pleiad. Looks like he's not breathing anymore." Eli smiled broader.

"What's wrong with you? Don't you care that he's dying? Help me!" She started CPR, unable to recall how many breaths went with each chest compression, vaguely recalling her Red Cross training from years ago. She compressed a couple of times and then breathed for him

Eli yelled, "Stop that CPR shit and do what you need to do!"

Kat took a deep breath and relaxed. Intuition encouraged her to rest her hands on his chest and then move them in a circular motion. No compressions. A buzzing rumbled in her ears. The hair on her arms stood erect. She thought desperately, *Don't die, Matt. Not yet. I don't trust anyone else in your world. I shouldn't trust you either, but I'm not quite ready to let you get out of the mess between us this easily. Besides I owe you one for healing me.*

Her hands burned and her world shifted like an elevator coming to a halt. On instinct she yanked the glass shard out of his arm. The wound bled, but not as brisk as expected for the wicked-long laceration. His chest rose as he sucked in air for the first time in minutes.

Her clinical mind assessed he'd been hypoxic for too long. Oxygen deprivation. He was likely to have brain damage, if he woke up. *Oh God, don't let him be a null stuck in this beautiful shell.*

A few seconds later his blue eyes popped open and connected with hers. "You okay?" he asked.

Whew, not a vegetable. She pulled her hands away from him. "Yeah. I'll be okay. But, you're a mess."

He massaged his forehead. "Those OLM guys are going to pay for this."

Obviously, he knew nothing of his near-death experience. She caught Eli's stare. His gaze was a clear what-the-hell-did-I-just-see. She silently pleaded with him to stay quiet. He nodded subtly at her.

Matt pulled himself up to look out the driver-side window. "Eli, you ready to fight? We don't have much time. What's her background story?"

Eli cleared his throat. "She was a vet in Virginia. Decided on a change of scenery and now works here. Grew up in Virginia. Went to that state school."

"I didn't go to Virginia," She interrupted, "I went to NC State. I don't know anything about that school."

"Fake it. No one else knows what it's like to be in vet school."

"I don't even know what city the school is in."

Eli sifted through rubble until he came up with a gun and murmured, "Thank God."

Matt shook his head as if fighting to stay conscious. "If they get you, try to shift back to your dimension. You got what Eli said? Stick to it."

"What is going on?" she asked, confused. "Are you leaving me?"

"Don't tell them anything. Don't show them anything. I mean don't do anything that's not *normal*. Stay alive. I'll find

you. Or Jason can find you."

"Who's Jason? You're not allowed to leave me!"

Before he could answer, the driver-side back door was wrenched open. Eli shot several rounds.

Matt shifted so that she was behind him, but the effect was crushing. She heard the grunts of him fighting but couldn't see anything.

Eli ordered, "Jump. Now, Kat."

"I can't do it on demand."

"We're not leaving you," Matt said.

Eli said, "This isn't about me. It's about the two of you. Go. Now."

Kat focused on her apartment and felt power within her swell. She knew it was going to work this time. She hugged Matt tightly, hoping he'd go with her. She couldn't leave him. He'd die here.

Chapter Sixteen

"Get off. Can't breathe," Kat choked out.

Matt rolled onto his side next to her. He cursed and threw his arm over his eyes. "What the hell did you do to me? My eyes… Did you blind me?"

She squinted into their surroundings. And blew out a relieved sigh when she recognized the less than pristine molding and early nineties white laminate countertops. "I brought you with me. This is my condo in my dimension." She tried to rev up enough energy to sit, but her muscles remained as coordinated as silly goo. Guess it took a bit more energy to jump two than one. A head roll confirmed they were mere feet from where her keys rested on the floor from their slip-n-slide off the counter.

"You what?" He sat upright and groaned. "Christ, my head's spinning. You go through this every time you dimension hop?"

"Yeah. Give it a minute. It'll pass."

"I thought jumping another person was supposed to be too dangerous. Thought it was banned."

"Like anyone told me the rules. By the way, you're welcome for saving your ass. I just wish I could've brought Eli, too. I hope he's okay."

"I'm the one who saved your ass. Eli's a survivor. There's not much we could've done if we'd stayed other than die." She detected the worry in his voice.

"I really hope he will be okay. Whoever was chasing us… I'm worried."

"A Sentry's vow is to protect you…any Pleiades, with his life." He pulled himself to a stand using the counter as leverage.

Her vision cleared and she stared at his black-jeans-clad calves. A droplet of his blood hit the floor near his shoe. Gingerly, she leaned forward and touched a wet, darkened area on his calf. He tensed. Her hand came away with blood. "Oh God. How bad are you hurt?"

"I'll be fine."

After an inelegant rise, she stumbled to her master bathroom, returning with her first-aid kit.

Matt eyed the Tupperware container she set on the kitchen table. "I'm fine."

She pursed her lips and raised her eyebrows in a silent, *really?* "Let me look at whatever's bleeding on your leg."

"Let's not and assume I'll heal."

"I know you've got some sort of ramped up super-healing ability, but I would prefer you stop hemorrhaging all over my floor. So, let me at least bandage it. Sit." She pointed at a kitchen chair.

He collapsed into the chair with a grunt.

She bit her lip against a smile when he glared at her stubbornly and declared, "Look, I really will be okay."

She knelt and rolled up his pants. Midcalf, a small hole leached blood. The opposite side of the muscle had a similar hole. "Looks like it passed through. That's good, I guess. I'm used to treating urban pets. I haven't seen more than maybe two bullet wounds in my career." She glanced upward to meet his gaze. "Thank you." Then she focused on the wound. The act of cleansing with peroxide and gauze almost distracted her mind from the horror of him taking a bullet for her and protecting her during the car accident. Efficiently, she placed gauze pads over the exit sites and rolled a bandage around his calf. Standing, she announced, "That ought to hold for a while."

"Thanks." He righted his pants leg.

"Is that the only place they got you?" she asked.

Matt glared.

"That's a no. Where else?"

"Forget about it."

With hands on her hips she ordered, "Show me where else."

He muttered, "Stubborn." And pulled up his T-shirt to expose a bloody area on his right side beneath his ribs.

She frowned. "That's got to hurt." Gently, she cleaned away the crusted blood and then probed. "I think this one went through, too." She put an extra-large Band-Aid over both the entrance and exit areas and replaced his shirt. Pleasure exploded in her chest at being able to care for him. She raised the sleeve of his left arm and ran her hand over the gash surrounded by crusted blood. "You almost died."

"No I didn't."

Her gaze shot upward, uncertain what would greet her. His fathomless eyes met hers. She said, "After the car stopped rolling, I pulled a huge piece of glass out of here while you were unconscious. The glass almost cut through your arm."

His gaze shot to the wound. "You pulled glass out of there?" He ran his hand over the area that now resembled a superficial gash. "It should've bled…a lot. And if that was deep enough to hit the major vessel, then when you removed it there would've been no stopping the bleeding." His gaze snapped to hers. "Did you do something to me?"

She nodded and stared at the gash as the horror of his almost death crashed in. She needed Matt in a way that terrified her. Needed him to help her navigate the dangers of his dimension, and help her understand the dimension hopping. Beyond that she needed him on a soul-deep level that she'd denied for years, but now recognized as inescapable. "You stopped breathing. You really were on the way out."

He lifted her chin to look deeply into her eyes. Softly he asked, "What happened?"

"Eli pushed me to help you by following my instincts. I'm not really sure what I did, but I didn't want you to die. I think we shared energy or something. One minute you were almost gone. I freaked out. Eli yelled at me. And the next minute you miraculously woke up. You seriously didn't breathe for longer than a minute or two. Your brain should've been damaged from low oxygen, but you woke up fine."

• • •

Oh my holy fucking God repeated over and over in Matt's brain. She'd done a magical heal on him like he'd heard rumors bonded pairs could do when the other faced death from injury.

Matt caught her as she stood, pulling her into his lap. With his free hand, he slid his fingers into her hair and cupped her jaw. Everything about her enthralled him, from the tiny freckles over the bridge of her nose, to her dilated green eyes that zeroed in on his lips. His need for her pulsated against his zipper. He wanted to feel her surround him. Perhaps that would erase the fear of her almost getting kidnapped and the panic over them possibly being destined. Nothing would ever assuage his terror that she'd get hit when bullets started flying.

"Are you sure you're not hurt? No bullets hit you? No major hurt from the car crash?"

"I'm fine. No bullet wounds." Her sensual lips parted, and he could've sworn she leaned closer to him. Those lips now rested inches from his. Tempting.

He asked, "Can you read my thoughts? They…the druids said that's probably your gift."

She shook her head. "I get something from everyone else. But nothing from you."

He slowly smiled. "Nothing? Are you sure? You seemed to understand about me not being in love with my job unlike anyone else."

She shook her head. "Nada. That was a guess based on your expression. I'm pretty good at reading people's intentions after a few years as a vet."

"So you can't hear what I'm thinking right now?" He shouldn't start anything with her. He was humming with too much adrenaline and pent-up fury to be gentle.

"I wish I could. It would be easier to understand a lot of things about you, I suspect."

He traced her lips with a finger.

She jerked away. "What about your fiancée?"

"I'm not engaged. I asked Cindy to leave, which prompted her to say that bullshit. Then you popped away before we could talk." He resumed tracing her lips with a finger.

She whimpered and shattered his willpower. His mouth claimed hers in a burning rush. He took advantage of her parted lips to invade her mouth and then coax her tongue into a sinuous dance. He savored the feel of the heat at the vee of her thighs riding his erection. A moan detonated from his chest when her fingers teased the circlets of his nipples through his shirt. He needed to ensure she would never forget what he felt like inside her.

As his hand smoothed down her ribs toward the edge of

her shirt, she winced. He broke the seal of his mouth on hers and tugged up her shirt, which exposed a wide bruise over her ribs. The need to annihilate every last member of the OLM consumed his mind. Hoarsely he choked out, "You *are* hurt."

"It's nothing. Must've happened when the car rolled. I'm fine." She cupped the back of his head and pulled him to her lips.

She fisted his T-shirt in one hand and pulled it upward. "Take this off," she pleaded. He broke the kiss.

"Sweetheart, I want to go there, but we both need a shower first. I need to get rid of the smell of blood." *And ensure you're not injured elsewhere.*

She ran her hand beneath his shirt over his abdomen toward his pants. "Make this a together event?" She lifted her eyebrows. Those puffy recently kissed lips curved upward.

He gritted his teeth. Now he was as hard as he could be. He choked out, "Lead on." He followed into her modest bedroom, noticing the framed items over a pressboard desk. Veterinary school diploma. Bachelor's degree. Three certificates that had silhouetted dancing couples. There was a picture of a happy middle-aged couple. "Those your parents?" They couldn't be her real parents, not in this dimension.

Her gaze darted to the picture. She nodded and massaged her forehead.

"What's wrong?" he demanded.

"Was thinking of them…my parents, or at least the ones who adopted me, and now my head is killing me."

He framed her face with his hands and sent a jolt of healing into her. "Better?"

She nodded. "Thanks. Bathroom's through here."

She led him into a white-tiled room with a standard shower-tub combination. Functional, but not sexy, not that he cared so long as their clothes were coming off. She started the water. Without a word, she turned and slid out of her clothes. The breath slammed out of him as he gazed at the flawless skin of her back, the graceful line of her spine and the flare of her hips. One hooded backward glance and then she disappeared behind the shower curtain.

Naked happened in seconds. He stepped behind the curtain and leaned down as she strained upward. He kissed her with every bit of the passion and possession thrumming in his blood. He pulled her flush to him, his erection cradled between them. His voice came out raw, gritty. “I’m not sure what you do to me, but…”

He winced when she ripped off the now drenched bandage on his side.

She said, “Sorry. Should’ve warned you. You forgot about these. We’ll need to replace them.” She ran her hand along the almost healed area where he’d been shot. “Or maybe not. That’s amazing.” She knelt and removed the bandage around his calf, finding a likewise almost healed area.

He tugged her upward and smoothed her wet hair away from her face. “All I’ve thought about since you disappeared is touching you, being inside you. I’m sorry about Cindy. She wanted to hurt you.”

“She did a good job, then.”

“Forget her.” His lips brushed hers. He kissed along her jawline and smoothed his hands down her back, over the flare of her hips. “Tell me what you want.”

“I think we should start with shampoo.”

He chuckled and reached behind her for the bottle. “Wet your hair for me, wildcat.”

She arched her head backward into the spray, running her hands through the now darkened strands. Had there ever been anything more erotic? Unable to resist he leaned in and kissed her neck.

She gasped and jumped.

Quickly he washed his own hair and rinsed. Then he

slowly massaged shampoo into her scalp. He worked his hands down her neck and spine.

Her eyelids drifted closed with a moan. "That's amazing."

"Wait until we get to soaping. Rinse your hair."

She rinsed while he popped open the body wash. He worked some into a lather between his hands. Quickly he washed himself. Then he stroked from her shoulders in gentle massaging to each breast and then down her abdomen. When he reached the bruise over her side and stomach, he slowed and released his healing energy.

"Why does it feel so warm?" She glanced down. "Are you doing your thing again?"

He nodded.

"Doesn't it require your own energy? At least, that's what Eli said."

"Mmm-hmm," he mumbled.

"Stop. You need all the energy you've got for yourself. You got more dinged up than me. I'll be fine."

He laughed. "Didn't I say something like that a few minutes ago?"

She smiled. "Be careful for yourself."

"Wildcat, you've got nothing to worry about." His healing power assured him she was to a safe, pain-free state, not that he'd ever understood how exactly he knew. He just knew. He resumed washing her upper body. Unable to resist he leaned in and kissed along one breast, tugging gently on the nipple. She cried out and gripped his shoulders.

Her hand closed tightly around his cock. With a moan she said, "Please. I need you."

"You're in such a hurry," he murmured as he moved over to the other breast. He detected a fine tremor in her body. He teased the junction of her thighs with his fingers, drifting a finger over her clit, and then across her wet folds, drawing a moan from her. He covered her lips with his again and consumed her next sobbing breath. She released him to dig her nails deeply into his back when he tunneled his fingers into her clenching sex. Whimpering into his mouth, she rode his thrusting fingers. He teased her clit with gentle motions until she came with a keening cry, her core milking his fingers.

"Damn," he exhaled. He supported her now boneless weight as her body vibrated with aftershocks. God, he wanted to be there, to feel her surrounding him.

"That was incredible," she said. "Now I'm not kidding. I need you. Inside me."

He picked her up and out of the shower. After a quick towel dry, he led her into the bedroom. He kissed her hard and backed her up until she fell onto the bed. He covered her with his body and resumed kissing.

A distant pounding distracted him. "What is that noise?"

"What noise?" she asked, pushing up onto her elbows.

A loud pounding on the front door was punctuated by a yell.

"Someone's at the front door, and I think I know who." She pushed out of his arms and pulled a towel around her.

A man yelled through the door, "You better be in there, Kat. Missing two days at work without so much as a text is annoying. Don't you dare stand me up."

"Who the hell is that?" Matt asked as he wrapped a towel around his waist. Who the hell would she be greeting naked at the front door?

"Riley. Oh God, it can't be Saturday. I forgot." She twirled a second towel onto her head.

Matt retrieved his knife from his discarded pants and shot upward. If Riley was a boyfriend, he'd kill him.

Quickly she added, "Good-guy team."

"Your team?" His lips thinned.

She rolled her eyes. "I work with him. He's a vet, too, but I've got this thing today with him. We're supposed to go somewhere, but I'm not sure. With you here…let me see what we can work out. Put that knife away. You'll terrify him."

"What kind of *thing*?" he demanded, unwilling to relinquish the weapon.

She didn't answer as she pulled open the door.

"Ah. Caught you in the shower." The guy strolled in, obviously familiar with the place. He slung a garment bag over a kitchen chair. His gaze shot to Matt. "Oh. You've got company."

Matt locked gazes with the interloper. Stats were measured and probabilities calculated. A once-over of the guy's light purple polo shirt and skintight slacks ensured him that Riley had no concealed weapons. The pristine arrangement of his hair and powerful cologne finalized his decision that Riley wasn't interested in Kat for sexual reasons, which was a good thing. He lay his knife on the kitchen table. A subtle threat.

"Stand down, boys. I don't need a testosterone face-off right now. Matt, this is Riley. He's a work colleague, and not your competition. He's a good *friend*. Riley, this is Matt and he's—"

"Your time-travel hotness?" Riley interrupted and did an up-and-down on Matt, ending in a grin. "Twenty? Honey, I would've given him at least a twenty-five. I mean that…" He waved at Matt's chest. "Is worth at least five points."

Her already pink, recently orgasmed cheeks blushed darker. "Yeah, okay. But, seriously, I do not time travel. We, uh, had a bit of a problem in Matt's dimension."

"What's this about twenty?" he asked, resisting the urge to grin.

Her face turned a darker shade of red.

"What kind of trouble?" Riley asked.

"Bad guys shot at us. But we're fine." Her gaze darted to Matt's healing side.

"Since you're not mortally injured, you and I are going to

do this event. You may be quitting at the clinic, or might even get fired if you miss more work, but I'm going to have to keep my job for the foreseeable future. So, get dressed."

"What about Matt?"

Riley squinted at him and worked his lower jaw.

She met Matt's dark gaze. "Would you like to come with us? It's a reception."

"I'm going wherever you go," he stated. He wouldn't let her out of his sight.

She frowned. "We'll need to get you a tux. I don't think there's any way we can stuff you into one of Riley's."

"Probably not." He enjoyed the renewed color in her cheeks that he knew had everything to do with remembering where they'd left off.

Riley said, "We'll stop at a rental place on the way, and see what they have in stock that fits. It's last minute, so you might get stuck with a baby-blue ruffle special."

He infused the Voice into his reply. "No ruffles."

Riley took a step back. "We can stop at more than one place if the first doesn't have something acceptable."

At least his ability worked in this dimension. He asked Kat again, "What sort of thing do you have to do?"

"Let's get dressed." Without further explanation, she disappeared into her bedroom.

Chapter Seventeen

Matt hadn't complained through the five suits he'd tried and modeled. Each one was tight in the wrong spots—arm, legs, chest. The store manager claimed he wasn't a shape this rental place dressed often. She thought it an excuse that gave the manager a chance to touch him in all the spots that lacked the flab of his normal customers.

He rotated in the mirror, modeling suit number six, and subtly frowned. The store manager groaned and plucked at his tie. She smiled at the little salesman's desperation to please Matt. The guy had an obvious monster crush on him. And who wouldn't?

Each time he emerged from the small curtained off changing area, he'd looked spectacular. She'd just finished concocting an X-rated fantasy of him removing the last tux behind that thin curtain, and her body was on fire. The subtle friction of her thighs was almost enough to make her come. But the imagery of him naked behind that curtain tortured her. She imagined him taking her in that small space. Although her body wanted her to act out that fantasy, it scared her, realizing she needed so much from him. And wanted so much more than he was probably willing to give.

The salesman said, "I think I've got one more that you can try, sir."

"This one is fine. I'll take it."

"Oh, bless the Lord. Let me draw up the paperwork. I'll be right back."

Riley nodded. "It'll work. I need to hit the john before we head out."

Matt draped the suit jacket over a chair and plopped down on the bench beside her. The thin fabric of her scoop dress provided little barrier from the rub of his solid, muscular thigh against hers. Her body tingled with awareness. She swallowed hard, probably too loudly but didn't care.

Hoarsely she said, "Thanks for putting up with this. That one looks a little tight, too."

"The suit will work. Did you enjoy the show?" The backs of his knuckles brushed against her cheek as he gazed down. His eyes flickered with passion and promise. For a second she recognized in his gaze the same confusing emotion she felt whenever in his presence.

"You drive me crazy, Kat. Most of these suits don't fit in *certain* places because I want to do whatever is running through your brain every time I tried a new suit."

"I didn't mean to make you crazy," she rushed out, her voice breathless. She struggled to keep her gaze on his face and not glance down. If she did, she'd want to touch. And probably drag him behind that curtain.

"You've got to stop looking at me like you'd be happier if I ripped off these clothes. Or yours. Riley seems to be in a hurry to shuttle us to this event. But right now I'm more inspired to stay here." He leaned in and whispered into her ear, "I'll bet I can convince you my idea of where we should go would be far more satisfying."

Oh God. Her mind replayed her dressing-room fantasy. "I'm sorry. I just…I don't understand anything when it comes to you."

He said, "You and I need to talk about many things."

So true. "Are you truly not marrying Cindy?"

He laughed a deep, brief laughter than made her stomach flutter. He shook his head. "You're still worried about that? We just had a crash and got shot at, leaving Eli to God only knows what fate. We did a dimension shift, which was insanely risky. And you're still worried about Cindy?"

"On my priority list it ranks number one. I mean, I am grateful. Thank you for everything. But she mentioned a Rome wedding…"

"I never had plans to marry her. We never had a future. She was talking pure bullshit."

"Was that before or after we collided at that benefit that the two of you have no future?"

"Long before, but seeing you again confirmed that relationship was over. Let's not talk about her again." His heated gaze scorched downward to her gown's plunging neckline. He flashed a meaningful smile that left no doubts as to exactly what he wanted.

Momentarily she forgot what they'd been speaking about. Her heart beat wildly.

The salesman rushed in and required Matt sign papers to rent the tux. He buzzed away.

Softly she asked, "What about your first wife? Online it said you separated and then she committed suicide, but at the benefit the other night someone mentioned you killed her."

His eyes swirled with sadness. "Rumors are a terrible thing. The official report was drug overdose, but she never did drugs. No doubt she was high-strung, and we were on the road to divorce, but I never hurt her. I barely touched her the last two months of our marriage before she moved out. And then she was murdered. It didn't work with us. I couldn't give her what she wanted other than my money, and she went a little crazy. I'm pretty sure the OLM kidnapped her. That type of death is their MO, but I have no proof."

"That's awful. I'm so sorry." She placed a hand on his forearm. "So, what's the deal with us? Me bouncing into your world and…well, frankly, I don't really understand any of this. Eli mentioned something about Pleiades."

"With you and me, I—"

"All righty folks, lets head out," Riley interrupted. He rotated his watch and grimaced. "I'm driving, and we're going fast."

• • •

Kat stood next to Matt at the edge of the reception dance floor, sipping champagne. At least a million bucks must've been laid out for this wedding and reception, probably more. The magnificent ice sculpture, recreations of a Michelangelo, and the cake, which had to be at least six tiers of gold-crusted leaves and fondant were definite wows.

Matt's rented tux wasn't the quality of the one she'd seen him in at the benefit, but no one noticed clothes when it came to him. Every female in the vicinity kept vying for his attention. Women shot him ocular come-ons that made her feel as inadequate as a middle schooler at a high school prom. How could she possibly keep his interest long-term with this kind of competition?

"I'm glad you're here," Kat said softly to him.

A half smile curved his lips as he glanced around. "This is not exactly how I envisioned spending my weekend. But, at least I can get a drink at this party." He raised his glass of scotch and sipped. "So, why are we here? These don't really seem like your people."

"Who exactly do you think my people might be?"

Riley cut off his reply. "They're ready for us, Kat. But before we go do that, and before you pop out of this world to take him home, I want you to promise me something. Promise no matter what happens, you will always make it for rehearsals on Thursday and do the major competitions every year." He shuffled his feet and glanced at the floor. "I get the feeling you're going to be more interested in going wherever it is you go instead of here."

She hugged Riley and kissed his cheek. Stepping back, she noticed Matt scowling. "Of course, but I'm not going to another Wiccan thing. That is not for me."

Riley broke into a huge grin. "Great. It's time to get ready." He paused, caught in Matt's glower. "Didn't you tell him what we're doing?"

She squeezed Matt's hand. "It's nothing bad. I just wasn't sure how you'd take this, but I've got to go do this thing with Riley. It should take a few minutes to prep, a few to do, and then I'll be done."

He asked far too calmly, "What exactly are you doing?" His blue eyes warned her he was at the edge of his tolerance for mystery.

Riley laughed. "Maybe this should be a surprise. She's really extraordinary."

Matt's scowl deepened.

"I'm going to dance with Riley and do a little demo for everyone. That's it."

"Dance? You can't. Not in public."

She laughed. "Says who? Just give me a few minutes. Trust me, we're good." She slipped off with Riley.

• • •

Dance? Pleiades were forbidden to do anything other than

stiff social dance in public. Matt had never seen a Pleiades really let loose, but according to Quinn it had the effect of making everyone watching so hot for sex that it was like throwing a match onto dry pine needles during a drought.

He should stop whatever was about to transpire. Just as his legs moved to take him in the direction she'd disappeared, the background music stopped.

The bride stood with microphone in hand. "Friends, family, welcome to our celebration. To get this party started I'd like to introduce this year's National Amateur Latin Dance Champions: Riley Levine and Katherine Ramsey. My multitalented veterinarians."

The lights dimmed. Sultry Latin tones filled the room. He tried to suck in air when Kat and Riley dance-walked onto the floor. She wore a green sequin-and-fringe outfit that showed far more skin than it covered. The fabric stretched tight to her curves when her hips started to rotate. The slit up her right leg went right up to… *Holy hell*, was she even wearing anything underneath? She kicked one of her heels in a way that made it obvious she was wearing something beneath, but the scant strip of green fabric revealed more secrets than he wanted any other man in this room seeing.

Riley wore a matching skintight, green, synthetic outfit with a shirt that was open until it tucked into his waist. Riley's slim body was as limber as silly putty. He rolled his hips in a way that must've taken decades to perfect. He spun her, and that was when Matt realized there was no back to her dress. It went from a small spaghetti shoulder strap to her waist, showing off her elegant spine. Her red hair whipped across that expanse of naked skin in a ponytail of waves to her midback.

The two of them pelvis rolling through what he identified as a samba was like watching dancing sex. Quinn had been right. Riley was but an accessory. She was the show. Electric and erotic. Yet, she was elegant and hauntingly beautiful. His gut demanded he yank her off the floor and throw his jacket over her. But, he couldn't move, let alone breathe. He was as spellbound as the entire audience, watching her. His body recognized this sultry witch on an elemental level. Blood surged to his groin.

He usually rolled his eyes at the calculated, showy way most pro dancers moved. These two made it look effortless and liquid. Watching her provoked his body into a heady mixture of jealousy and arousal.

Riley dipped her so low that her head almost hit the floor. From her upside-down position, her eyes found his.

In that moment, he realized there would never be another woman for him, regardless of whether she had or had not cursed him to dissatisfaction with every other woman. He'd tried to make do with look-alikes for a decade, but none had been her. Hell, he'd lost his soul to her the moment he'd found her at his frat party in college, even though he'd handled the morning-after part abysmally.

Somehow, he would convince her to be his. And to stay in his dimension. This would involve some dramatic life changes for him, but his life needed a makeover. This level of permanence cramped his gut with unease, but he wouldn't allow another druid to claim her.

Shit, shit, and super shit. That meant he'd have to deal with Bryce and his bullshit long-term. He could no longer run from his heritage.

Riley threw Kat into a dip and fast twirl. His breath caught, fearing she'd fall. She smiled and the two promenaded off the floor with synchronized hip rotations. She was magnificent.

And she was his.

Chapter Eighteen

"What'd you think?" Kat asked.

Matt jumped.

She bit back a smile, pleased that she'd surprised him. She couldn't read anything from him. Hopefully, she hadn't shocked him too much.

"You guys were…pretty good," he said noncommittally.

"Pretty good? I guess I'll take that for now, but I think we were better than that."

"You're not supposed to dance in public as a Pleiad. It's forbidden because of…that." He waved at the dance floor.

"I don't know what being a Pleiad means. What was so wrong with it? That took years of practice and a lot of competitions."

His gaze raked her outfit. A flush highlighted his cheeks. He pulled her tight to him, and there was no question his southern hemisphere was jacked up. "It's too much for most people to take, watching you move like that."

"Was it too much for you?" she asked.

He pulled her down a hallway and whirled her into a

dark, deserted closet. His mouth covered hers.

She slid her fingers through his hair, the soft strands making her fingers tingle. She loved his unique taste—wild aroused male mixed with Scotch. That, in combo with the endorphin high still circulating in her blood, had her teetering on the edge of wild abandon.

His stiff arousal pushed between her legs while his tongue swept her mouth.

A riptide of lust seized her, sweeping away insecurity and worry about the future. And blinded her with desperation to have him inside her. Maybe that could cool the fever of lust that burned only for him. A low moan slipped past her lips—a husky and helpless sound of need. *Oh God. Yes.*

He lifted to balance her against the wall, grinding his rigid erection against the scant underwear covering her core, which was already drenched for him. Damn him for being like no other—hard, ruthless, and dominant. Damn her traitorous body for desiring only him.

She reached for the fastening of the tuxedo trousers, freeing him. He groaned when she palmed him, and caught her mouth in another deep kiss that swallowed her answering moan. He slid her skirt up her thighs, bunching the fabric in his hand. And fingered aside the wet panties to swirl around her clit. One more pass and she'd explode. But those too-knowing fingers didn't make that pass. Disappointment soared as she reached for that release.

"Please, Matt."

"Please what?"

"Stop teasing. I need you inside me."

He worked off her panties and then repositioned between her legs. He pushed into her slowly—thick, hot, and so hard. Her fingers dug into his biceps as she tried to wriggle to get him to move, to lose control and stop the torment. But his hand clamped her hip and held her in place.

He broke from her lips and whispered, "You shall suffer a bit for what you just put me through."

"You're killing me. Matt…please."

He moved just a little deeper, the sensation setting off nerve ending explosions. "Here?" he asked. And then he moved a little deeper, nudging the section deep inside that sucked the air from her lungs. Fireworks exploded in her brain. Her wild cry gave him his answer.

He chuckled and flexed his hips in what wasn't so much a thrust as an internal rub. Ruthlessly he stroked that deep zone.

She cried out again under the onslaught of intense pleasure. Her body clenched and convulsed on that edge, but she couldn't quite get there. She begged, "Please…I can't take this."

"You can take it."

She tried to move, to incite him to lose this vicious control he had, but he locked her pelvis and tortured her with another deep stroking.

Desperate to move, she sank her teeth into his shoulder.

He growled, and his body bowed. His control shattered. After several hard thrusts, her body clamped down and her mind exploded.

She was only dimly aware of the power of Matt's convulsions as he pumped violently into her.

In the silent afterward, reality returned in bits. First, awareness of a dark closet lit only by light sneaking under the door, and the assortment of mops and buckets surrounding them.

Slowly he withdrew and pressed a cloth she suspected was his handkerchief between her legs, absorbing the wetness he'd left.

They both slowly straightened clothes, while thoughts of *that'd-been-great-but-nuts* swirled in her brain. And yet again, they'd forgotten protection. She needed to reiterate to him her inability to take birth control pills. Even so, the thought of another baby, his baby, didn't bother her. That spooked her.

The world went blurry and started to teeter.

"We're going back." She quickly righted her clothes and then clung tight to him.

Chapter Nineteen

"I'm never getting used to the eyes burning part of this," Matt grumbled.

Kat stumbled, blind and off-balance, reaching out for anything solid. His arm wrapped her waist and anchored her to his side. She leaned into him with a relieved sigh, impressed that he didn't waver despite the fact he had to be fighting the same mental whirlybird that owned her mind.

She asked, "Where do you think we are?" Her head hurt too much to try to sense for thoughts or chance squinting for a visual.

"Looks like my house in the Hamptons. In the office."

"You think it's safe?" she asked. When he twisted as if glancing around, she gripped his arm.

He murmured, "I've got you. Can you see yet?" He enfolded her in his arms.

"No." She relaxed and rested her ear against his chest, comforted by the rhythmic rise and fall of his breathing.

He rubbed circles on her back.

"Mmm. That's nice."

Suddenly he stopped. His body snapped taut. "We're not alone. I'll handle this."

"Handle what?" She peeked through cracked eyelids. The light from the windows seared through her skull.

"I knew it would work," boomed a man with a Scottish accent. "I've never done a command summon on a Pleiad before, but this was getting ridiculous."

Her eyes finally decided they were on board with vision. Four large men blocked the office doorway. One glimpse of the Scott who made that declaration and pain lacerated her mind. Her knees buckled, but Matt caught her before she fell and locked her against him. She gripped her head, hoping whatever had her brain in a vise clamp would halt.

Visions of her real mother flashed in her head. The pictures included the Scott. She remembered him now. Bryce Sinclair.

Daddy.

Scattered images of him in her childhood replayed as if someone had opened a locked door to memoryville. Despite her excitement at remembering her real past, her head screamed agony while memories poured in.

"What's wrong?" she heard Matt ask, but his voice sounded faint and far away.

"Head," she choked out. "Hurts."

His large palm massaged the back of her neck. All head pain vanished. She took a deep breath and chanced an eyelid crack. No pain. Functional vision. He was her own personal miracle. She glanced up at him. "All gone. Thank you."

"Did one of them try to hurt you?"

She shook her head and took a step away from him. "I don't think so. I just remembered some of my childhood. I think it was memory overload."

The two hulking men beside her father grumbled low to each other. A college-aged guy stepped beside Bryce. And Eli, who she hadn't gotten a good look at before. Eli was the same height as Matt, and looked almost identical, except for the facial scar and different hair. His brother was a twin. Thank God he'd survived the earlier attack.

They had to be druids. That meant they could potentially hurt her using magic. A sudden surge of aggressive thoughts from the druids hit her frontal lobe. She staggered into Matt and groped for his hand.

"I don't recall inviting any of you to my house." He glared at his brother. "Eli. Are you taking sides?"

Eli shifted on his feet. "No. I am but concerned for your safety. And hers. My duty above all else is to ensure her survival."

Matt glowered.

"I don't recall discussing you get personally involved with her rescue. That wasn't part of the deal," Bryce said.

"What deal?" she asked.

Matt didn't reply.

Bryce said, "The deal we made where he brings you to me. What the bloody blazes are you wearing, Katherine?"

"Long time, no see, Dad." She experienced a fleeting nostalgic happiness at a reunion with her father. But terror that he or his friends might hurt Matt killed her joy.

"Dad?" Matt rounded on her. He pulled his hand from hers and stepped away. Betrayal etched his features.

"I didn't remember until right now. My mother might've memory suppressed me when she left me in our alternate. I was only ten. Since I can jump dimensions, I assume those people that shot her with a poison dart didn't reverse the poison." She sought Bryce's gaze and added sadly, "Or killed her?"

The sorrow on her father's face was enough of an answer. He wasn't at fault for separating them so long ago. Almost twenty years. A lifetime.

Then, she caught her father's thoughts. *I'll see that gigolo in hell before he touches her.*

She stepped close enough to Matt to be in contact. He must've sensed her fear since he didn't move away. But tension thrummed through him. She may not understand the undercurrents, but there was some deep, very bad history here. That aside, he'd made a deal with Bryce? What kind of deal? Was everything Matt had said and done just a con? She couldn't believe that. Just couldn't. It'd shatter her soul to think he'd gone so far just for a deal. He'd already inflicted so much damage on her heart that if she discovered his complicity in anything like that she wasn't sure she could recover.

She remembered his wrist tat. And now recognized it as the mark of a Sentry druid. That didn't mean she trusted him 100 percent with her heart. Her life, however, *that* she knew he'd keep safe. But was his concern about her safety only to complete whatever deal he'd brokered with her father? Or did it have to do with Sentry vows?

"I repeat, what are you wearing?" Bryce demanded.

"She's the National Amateur Latin Dance champion in her dimension. She's…" His eyes met hers and went smoky. "Well, she's a really good dancer."

Her cheeks burned at the compliment. Warmth tingled her insides.

"Pleiades are forbidden to dance in public," Bryce announced.

Just as she bristled to defend herself, the college-aged guy stepped forward. She caught some hazy naked images of her from his mind, in some very unoriginal positions, not that that kind of imagery from a barely postpubescent guy surprised her. He pulled her away from Matt and locked his lips onto hers. Revulsion hit hard. She bit his tongue when he tried to push into her mouth.

With a yelp, he pulled away. She palm struck his chin,

sending him reeling.

Matt pounced, landing the guy on the floor with a knee to his chest and his hands wrapped around the kid's throat.

"Release Jason," Bryce ordered.

Matt gritted out, "The asshole has no right—" He flew off Jason as if tackled by an invisible linebacker. He bounced on the floor and slid until his head smacked against the wall. Then he gasped and clawed at his chest as if an invisible pressure crushed.

"Stop it!" she screamed. She knelt beside him, desperate to help him. "What's wrong?"

Jason tugged her away from Matt. She struggled to get out of his grip.

"Knock it off, Bryce," Eli said.

Matt popped upright, took one gulp of air, and lunged for Jason. He landed a brutal hook to Jason's chin.

The kid stumbled backward, releasing Kat.

Matt threw Jason face-first into the wall. Jason rolled, exposing a bleeding gash on his head.

Matt stepped away. His head snapped around to pin Bryce. "I'm not fixing him. The next time he touches her, I'll kill him."

She pointed at Jason, who'd stumbled behind Bryce to rest against the wall. "What the hell was that?"

Jason massaged his throat and slid along the wall farther away from Matt. "Katherine? We're destined to be together."

"Who are you? There's no chance of us doing anything together other than this." She stalked to Jason and slapped him hard. She reached back to do it again, but Matt caught her hand and pulled her against him. And away from the druids.

He whispered to her, "He's dead if he touches you again. Don't give him the opportunity."

"I can't believe he did that."

"Remind me again and I'll kill him right now." His deep

blue eyes promised death.

"Step away from her, Matthew. Now," Bryce ordered.

She detected the energy notch up a few degrees in the room. Terror hit hard. In her mind she screamed, *Someone help me. They're going to hurt him.*

Within seconds she heard voices from several women. The most prominent asked, *What's wrong? Is this my lost sister?*

Who are you? Kat asked.

I'm Charlotte. I saw you at that Wiccan thing. I'm sorry if I scared you. You are one of us, a Pleiades. What's going on?

The Pleiades were able to connect mentally? Cool. And, she really might be one of them.

She thought back to them, *I'm at Matt's house in the Hamptons. Matthew Ryan. We were in my world and now suddenly here. I thought I was getting better at this jump thing. The druids here might hurt him.*

Did Bryce pull a command summon on you? Charlotte asked in a tone that suggested she would personally crush him, if so.

Kat replied, *Don't know. What's a command summon? I didn't try to jump. It just happened.*

Hang on, honey, I'll handle this.

Seconds later a cell phone's electronic chime shattered the tense silence. Bryce pulled it from his jacket. "Now isn't a good time, Charlotte..." His cheeks blazed red.

Charlotte's rant was audible to all, "Did you? Did you pull a command summon on her?"

"Yes," Bryce replied. He held the phone away from his ear. All could hear the ball-busting tirade. When it died down he said, "Okay." And handed the phone to Kat.

"Hello?"

"Listen, honey, if Bryce so much as twitches to do anything you don't want, use what you've got on him. Forget the fact he's your father. I never knew what your mother, bless her soul, saw in that overbearing prick. Just remember your gifts work ten times better in this world, the Sourceworld. And they work doubly so on druids. Well, except for your destined, who I suspect is Matthew. I think he's a good choice for you. He's got issues, but gracious he's hot."

Kat smiled at Matt. "He is that."

Matt's eyebrows rose.

"Bet he's a rocket in bed," Charlotte drawled.

She choked out a strangled sound. Her cheeks burned.

Charlotte chuckled. "I'll be there in an hour or so. We'll clear up some of the confusion. Your ability enables you to connect all of us. If you need us, just reach out again." Charlotte disconnected the call.

She handed back Bryce's phone. "She'll be here in an hour."

Bryce nodded.

"Please, stop threatening Matt."

Bryce narrowed his eyes on Matt. "How many times have the two of you crossed paths?"

Matt glowered a silent fuck-you.

"I think we've answered enough personal questions," Kat announced.

"I'll leave you alone until Charlotte arrives if you tell me how many times you crossed paths," Bryce demanded. Obviously he was used to being the super shit in charge.

Matt replied, "More than a few."

"Since when. How old?" Bryce asked.

"Fifteen," Matt replied.

"I don't remember you until college."

"Remember when you arrived wet and shivering? Said something about a boat explosion before you passed out."

"Yeah, it killed my adopted parents. But you…I don't remember you that time. I remember a kind man with a lot of facial scarring. I think he healed me when I woke up, but then I popped back to my world…dimension." She shook her head.

"You pretty much conked out and slept for ten hours straight that first time you appeared. That man was Quinn, my father. I didn't put all the visits together until after this last time you jumped away."

"Shit," Bryce mumbled. "Talk about catastrofucks." He rolled his eyes toward the ceiling and massaged his temple. He pointed at Matt. "You're not good enough for her."

Hurt shimmered in Matt's brilliant blues before it glazed into stoicism.

"Obviously, you don't know Matt very well." She marched toward the exit.

As she passed Bryce, he said softly, "He's not for you, Katherine. He'll never be able to commit to what you will need."

At the door, she pretended she hadn't heard those devastating words that confirmed the fear wedged deep into her chest. "Matt, could you please show me to a room that I might borrow? I'd like to shower."

He led her to a resplendent bedroom, different from the guest room she'd been in last time—spacious with panoramic windows and a monstrous sleigh bed. This had to be the master bedroom. His.

Kat kicked off her heels, angry at the unfairness of the world. She may not be able to get long-term with Matt, but she sure as hell was getting her money's worth out of right now. She unzipped. The green sparkly costume hit the floor followed by underwear. Buck naked.

She shot him a smile more brilliant that the midday sun. "Coming?"

By the time she saw his feet hit the tiled bathroom floor, she already had the shower steaming and was slipping beneath the streams of the triple jets. She'd almost given up on him.

When his hand touched the shower's glass door she said, "You might want to lose the tux."

He glanced down as if surprised.

He shrugged the jacket and shirt from the powerful width of his shoulders. Muscles rippled. The bullet wound on his side and the gash on his arm had smoothed over, completely healed. Amazing.

Her fingers itched to touch him, to follow that dark trail of hair that disappeared into the waistband of the trousers. He ripped at the pants, his long powerful legs drawing free.

Her lips parted to drag in a ragged breath. He stepped beneath the jets, crowding her in the small space. Dipping down, he captured her lips. The kiss started slow, teasing, but quickly took a sharp left into deep and desperate.

His expert hands massaged southward, hitting her most sensitive zones. Her muscles tightened, indicating just how much she wanted this.

She gasped against the pressure of his tongue circling her nipple. He murmured, "So beautiful."

"Matt…" Her head fell back against the shower wall.

He worked his way upward. She gazed into his eyes, which were now hooded with anticipation.

Her hands circled him.

He hissed as she tightened pressure and stroked.

She smiled wickedly and started her own southward descent. With a flick of her tongue she circled his tip. He let his head fall back with an agonized groan. After three long strokes along his length, she took as much of him as she could.

"Wildcat," he choked out, threading his fingers through her wet hair. She whimpered when he pulled her hair a little too tight. "Sorry," he whispered, loosening. "I can't stand it."

She smiled and repeated his words from earlier, "You can take it." Her tongue rolled around his shaft, teasing.

He growled and pulled her away. She glanced up,

questioningly. He hauled her to her feet. "I can't go slow right now. Later, you can have your way. And don't doubt I'll enjoy it. You're just too good." He lifted her by her waist and balanced her against the shower wall. In one quick thrust he speared into her. She cried out and wrapped her legs around his hips. Both of them held as tight as they could with the slippery water. He led a fast tempo, ending for her in a release that was part desperation, part ecstasy. As his climax arrived with a bellow, she swore she felt a part of him sink deep into her soul.

And knew she hadn't managed to do the same to him, which shattered her heart.

Afterward, as he washed her with liquid soap and a washcloth, she asked, "So, what are you? I need to hear it from you. I need to know."

"Druid. Sentry Druid or at least I was. I walked away a few years ago."

She nodded. "Thought so. And you had training?"

He paused in his sensual cleaning of her back and neck. "When I was young, my biological father, Quinn, appeared. He was a druid healer and Bryce's second in command."

"You didn't live with him?"

"I was left with my mother, who was married to Grant Ryan." His lips compressed tightly.

"The father who wasn't nice to you and owned the company?"

"Yes, him."

She played with the damp hair near his ear. "Why didn't your real father take you?"

"Don't know. Probably part of a deal with my mother. My brother went with Quinn."

"Your brother…you're twins. I was shocked when I saw Eli and realized there are two of you."

He captured her mouth. Her brain forgot everything

other than the swirling vortex of sensation created by his mouth and the downward exploration of his hands, which were slow moving toward her ass. He ended the kiss abruptly and growled, "There's only one of me."

She opened her eyes and bit her lip against a smile. "Yes. Only one of you. But you've got a brother that looks just like you."

"But he's not me."

"You think I want to jump into bed with Eli just because he looks similar to you?"

"Just for admitting you thought about it, I'll kill him the next time I see his ass lazing it up on my sofa."

She punched him playfully in the arm. "No you won't, even if he wasn't very helpful when you were unconscious. Is Eli still a druid? Why are you no longer a druid and how exactly do you walk away?"

He sighed. "Eli is an active druid. I walked away from Bryce, them…the whole business about nine years ago. After the OLM murdered Quinn."

"That was about the time when I found you in that place." She paused and lowered her voice. "What they did to you… I can't even imagine what they did to your father."

"You don't want to know. It was bad. The three of us were imprisoned there: Quinn, Bryce, and I. The things they did to Quinn made what they did to me seem trivial. Bryce forced me leave him there." His voice faltered and he let go of her before he said, "Forced me to let him die." His muscles tightened.

She turned and slid her arms around him. "I'm sorry you lost him."

He didn't hug her back. After a few seconds, she glanced up. His gaze was fixed straight ahead. Although the shower's streaming water masked his face, she was fairly certain tears leaked from his eyes. This wasn't a man that liked showing weakness. And probably despised what she saw now.

"You've got that amazing healing ability. Why didn't Bryce let you do your thing on Quinn?"

"Bryce said my talent wasn't developed enough. That I might've died. But I'd have preferred… Can we discuss something else?"

"All right. Let's talk about undergrad."

His head fell forward. "I'm sorry about that."

"I thought we had a pretty good night—"

"Pretty good? It was better than *pretty good*," he interrupted.

"Yeah, it was mind-blowing. But you pushed me out of your dorm room while your girlfriend ranted hysterics at you. I was naked!"

"You had a sheet."

She scowled.

He snapped his lips closed over his grin. "Sorry."

"You had a girlfriend. What kind of guy hooks up when he has a girlfriend?"

"I'd never done that…hooked up with someone I barely knew. I'd never cheated on a girl. Or pushed a girl out like that. It was a whole bunch of firsts for me. I was messed up and hung over. I'm sorry. As to the why I did it—why we ended up in bed—hell, wildcat, once we met leaving you alone wasn't an option. And it scared the hell out of me."

So true for her, too. The second he'd said hello, she could think of nothing other than seeing him naked, not that she'd ever done naked prior to that. "Did it even mean anything to you? Or was it just the alcohol?"

She strained to hear his reply.

"I searched for you for a long time. I thought it was because you cursed me and I needed you to reverse it. But after a while, it was more complicated. I wanted you. I didn't care as much about the curse, although I did blame you for…

when it wasn't good with other women. I eventually even married someone who looked like you. The marriage didn't work out because she wasn't you. So, yeah, that night meant a lot."

Her heart warmed. "Did you tell your wife about being druid?"

He shook his head.

"Did you plan to?"

"No."

"How did you hide that part of yourself? You use the ability all the time. I was suspicious after knowing you for twelve hours. Guaranteed if I lived with you for a few days, I'd have figured it out. I barely understand what I am, but magic is a huge and weird part of my life. I want whomever I'm with to know about it. If you had a child, he'd probably have some of your talents."

He pulled her against him. "You're right."

"Are you ashamed of your abilities?"

"No. They just remind me of…my father."

She whispered against his chest, "I'm sorry. I wish I could've met him. Well, I think I did meet him, but I wish I could meet him now." She traced the contours of his chest. "What's going on with you and…my father? Bryce."

"No offense, but Bryce is a real bastard most of the time."

"Are you just here with me as a part of whatever deal you made with him, even though it sounds like getting it on in the shower might be taking things a bit further than the bargain you struck?"

Matt calmly replaced the soap and washcloth but didn't reply.

"Please tell me what you want from me. Or what my father wants. I don't completely understand this thing between us, but I still want you so desperately right now that I'd probably give it to you, or speak to my father to get whatever you needed. You don't have to play games with me." *I need to know if what we've got is about us or my father.*

Matt's spine snapped straight. His gaze darkened. He curled his fingers around her forearm and pulled her out of the shower, hooking two towels on his way to the bedroom. He wrapped one towel around her and pulled the other around his waist. He pushed her to sit on his bed, her hair dripping rivulets that trekked between her breasts. He leaned in close. "Do I seem like someone who would whore to get what he wants? Do I seem that unscrupulous to you?"

"Matt, I didn't mean—"

"The hell you didn't. I made no *deal* with Bryce. I wouldn't fuck anyone for anything other than mutual pleasure. There isn't a thing your father could do for me other than back the hell off threatening my sister. Even then, I wasn't planning to do what he ordered, which was to bring you to him, unless that's what you wanted. I don't know what I would've done about his threat against my sister, but I'd have handled it."

Oh God, she'd hurt him. She sucked at this relationship thing, not that she'd had a lot of practice. "I'm sorry. I didn't know." She tried to reach for his face, but he ducked away from her hand.

For a moment he gazed at her chest. Color darkened his cheeks. She glanced down. Her breasts were compressed and pushed upward by the tightly wrapped towel. If it slipped a few millimeters, her nipples would pop out. He pushed away from the bed with a curse, pawed through a bureau drawer, and grabbed a pair of pants. Within seconds he was clothed. He turned as if to say something, but slammed his lips closed and stalked out of the bedroom.

Chapter Twenty

Kat squirmed in the too-tight rayon blend dress that the butler-caretaker, Sam, presented her within minutes of Matt's hasty departure. She stopped her hand's path to tug the top upward. Wouldn't help. She'd already tried at least ten times. The dress was intended for someone a little less busty.

She stared across the grandiose dining room table beyond Bryce, Eli, and Jason. She wondered how long they'd be stuck here, waiting. The wind ruffled the evergreens outside, swirling snow from their branches. *Don't look toward the door.* But her peripheral vision worked too well. Matt sipped a Perrier while gazing out the opposite window. His body radiated the fury of an incensed feral tiger. As she'd entered, his eyes had swirled with dark emotion when they bumped into hers and then darted away.

She shifted to alleviate the pressure in her lower spine. The rigid angle of the designer chair might be beautiful, but it did nothing for long-term comfort.

Bryce and Eli worked on their smart phones nonstop. Jason intermittently blew out agitated sighs and ran his hand over his swollen face. He grumbled to Bryce about having better things to do. One glare from Bryce and all complaints ceased.

"Sit down," Bryce snarled at Matt.

Matt flashed him a glower and ignored him.

She'd screwed up, but in the long run maybe this was best. She and Matt wouldn't work, no matter what druids or other Pleiades thought. Sure the sex was amazing, but where could they go from here? He didn't want long-term. She wasn't into sharing when it came to him. And she could barely contemplate him dumping her. Once she fulfilled her obligations in this dimension, she'd return home where she'd stay. Far away from Matt. If Charlotte could bounce into her world, then she could notify when an appearance was required.

Panic squeezed her chest at the thought of never seeing him again, of him turning to another woman. In that moment she knew she'd made a drastic mistake. A horrible, irreversible mistake. She loved him.

She braved a glance his way. His arctic gaze narrowed. He turned his back to her.

Tears burned her eyes. Dragging in a hard breath, she struggled to remain seated. She wanted to rush out of this room and find a dark corner for some Niagara Falls action.

The tinkling of crystal announced Charlotte's arrival. A strikingly handsome man followed Charlotte into the dining room.

"How're you doing, Brian?" Bryce called out.

Brian waved, slouched against the doorframe and winked at Charlotte. She gazed up adoringly at him, then turned to face the rest of the room, very serious. She oozed power and confidence. After one directed glance at everyone in the room, she fanned the neckline of her gauzy dress and declared in a thick Southern drawl, "It's hotter in here than a goat's ass in a pepper patch."

Kat's lips twitched. Bryce rolled his eyes heavenward. Eli and Jason smiled.

Charlotte's eyes connected with Brian, who Kat assumed was Charlotte's husband. The man's hard face softened. Kat opened her mind to catch his thoughts. *God, she's spectacular.*

Her heart squeezed. She wanted that.

Bryce said, "Charlotte, I needed her here—"

Charlotte held up a hand, silencing him. "Don't you ever command summon one of us again. And I mean never ever. *Ever*. That could've resulted in a horrid incident. Imagine the mess if she'd been in a public situation. She'd become her dimension's newest miracle."

"I knew the risks. That's why I didn't try it until now. I could've done it at any time in the past two decades. But we need her here."

Charlotte pursed her lips and gave a small headshake and eye roll that translated into: *idiot.* "She jumped with Matthew Ryan, didn't she?"

Bryce folded his hands in front of his massive chest. And nodded.

"Christ Almighty, Bryce, sometimes I think God passed you over when it came to giving out good sense."

Bryce's voice dropped. "Maybe I should've been patient. Maybe I should've asked you."

Charlotte's expression softened as she moved toward Kat. "Welcome. I know it's been a bumpy beginning with us losing you in your alternate for so long. Then with Bryce doing this crazy thing. But my goodness, you're the spitting image of Lynn." *I need you here with your head in the game.*

Another person with an agenda. *Great.* Was there anyone that didn't want something from her? She nodded at Charlotte in greeting, but remained silent.

Charlotte caught Kat's left wrist and smiled. She met

Bryce's gaze and announced, "He marked her. Fabulous."

Bryce's face splotched red as he stalked to Matt and grabbed his wrist. "You did what?" He raised Matt's wrist into view and demanded of Kat, "Do you have this on your wrist?"

She nodded and exposed the mark.

Matt met Bryce's gaze head on and gritted out, "It was a mistake."

Bryce pushed away from Matt and thundered, "A mistake? That's beyond a juvenile fuckup. You have no right."

A mistake? That hurt. Matt didn't want her. She dabbed a finger at the moisture collecting the corners of her eyes.

Charlotte commanded, "Everyone leave us. Now." Several seconds later she said, "You too, Matt. Get out. Don't you be throwin' eyes at me." The second he left, she said, "Oh, honey. Tell me what's got you worked up. I can tell you're a mess," Charlotte said.

She wasn't about to reveal what really had her upset. "I don't know much of anything about all this. My mother must've marooned me in the other world…" She trailed off, not sure where to go.

"And you survived. That's the most important part. I am sorry you didn't get to know her better. Lynn was a beautiful soul. And, gracious, did that woman adore you. But it's not loss of her that has you so upset right now, is it?"

I screwed up with Matt. "I'm just overwhelmed."

"Sure." She drawled out the word with more than a minor hint of skepticism. "If it's got anything to do with one Mr. Matthew Ryan, then, honey, let me tell you that man has got issues, no doubt. But the boy has got it bad for you. You should've seen the moony eyes he threw your way when I arrived. I've been around the block and seen a lot of Pleiades find their man. The thing not to forget is that he walked away from us a few years ago. I don't think he wants to come back.

He also grew up knowing each of us usually has one Sentry that's our destined. That scares the bejesus out of all those boys. I think they each pray to never be *chosen.*"

"Why?"

"Fear. They're terrified of being united with a powerful woman who is hunted in this dimension by the OLM. They fear being stuck with that one woman for the rest of his life, and have the responsibility of producing a female child to carry on her line. And protecting that child. That's a lot for any man to come to grips with. He might be pissed at the semantics of this situation right now, but he'll come around. They all do. So…what do you modern kids say? Chill out? Getting them in the bedroom helps them come around to accept destiny. I think we already established that you and he already…" She quirked a meaningful eyebrow.

Kat blushed. The conversation had all the awkwardness of a sex conversation with her ultraconservative aunt. "Yeah."

"Then he ain't gonna be tomcatting around. Trust me. Let's get through this weekend."

"You make it sound as if this is all so easy."

"Easy? Nothing about you and him will be easy. You've got your father to contend with, who harbors some major ill will toward Matt. That man can be butt stubborn. Matt despises Bryce and has the same ass-stubborn streak. The two of them are alike, now that I think about it. Yep, that guarantees some family fireworks at get-togethers." She broke into a wide grin. "But we've got skills, honey. You proved you got the mental thing your mother did by connecting all of us. Only you can do that. That mental skill works doubly strong here, in this dimension. So, use it on the boys when they get out of line. Might not work well on Matt if he's your destined as I suspect. But it'll work enough. Just remember, when all else fails, get him in bed." She winked.

Kat didn't think her face could get any hotter. Desperate

to change the topic she asked, "What's your power? Aren't all of us different?" *And what do you want with me?*

"There are seven of us. Seven Pleiades. I told the story at that Wiccan meeting. I'm an elemental, which means I can command elements. Wind, fire, water. And I can go to all the dimensions."

"That'd be pretty cool. How many dimensions are there?" asked Kat.

"Cool, but the travel thing is confusing. There are seven dimensions. Each is similar, but not the same as I'm sure you discovered."

"If we're witches, can we do witchy things like wiggle our noses and get a wish?"

Charlotte laughed. "Wouldn't that be nice? But, no. We are each born with one unique talent. Christians labeled us witches, but our ancestors were simply the children of gods. Demigods, I guess you'd call them. Now our line is a bit diluted and all we retain of godly status is the abilities."

"Seems a bit far-fetched."

"It is what it is." Charlotte settled into the seat next to hers. "Let's talk about this weekend. We've got to fly tonight since we need to be in Ireland tomorrow. Most of the others are already on the way."

"Ireland?"

"Hate to get serious on you, honey, but this is the one thing that you must do as the representative of your line. Samhain is tomorrow. If you remember the story, every twenty years we have to convene to assure the veil between this world and the World of the Ancestors remains intact. The veil between our world and the world of the gods thins on Samhain, and the original seven must be reassured that their legacy continues. If not, then those original deities might cross, and in fury destroy our boys for failing to protect us, and then allow chaos to reign in the world. Armageddon-type stuff from that point."

Kat couldn't come up with a logical reply. This was all too much. She just couldn't be *that* important.

Charlotte clucked while glancing down. "Gracious, girl. Who gave you that dress?"

"I kind of popped over here without any luggage. Matt had this in his closet." The last part came out in a very sour tone. She didn't want to consider who wore it last and why it was still in his closet.

"We will have to fix this clothes situation. You can't run around in a sundress. It's freezing outside. You look pretty close to my daughter in size." She plucked a cell phone from a mysterious pocket in her gauzy dress and hit a few buttons before putting it to her ear. "How's my baby doing?" There was a long pause. "Oh, honey. I'm looking forward to seeing you. I need a little favor for Katherine. Yeah, Bryce's daughter is back. She's over here without any clothes... No, she's not naked, but she might as well be in the getup they found for her. You think you can meet us at the airport with some items? I think she's your size, if not a few inches shorter... You're a gem, sweetie. See you in a few hours." She kissed into the phone and hung up. With a brilliant smile she announced, "Problem solved. Now, tell me what you've been doing for twenty years."

• • •

Matt gave up pacing to recline on the love seat across from Bryce in the sunroom. Jason and Eli had departed under orders to prepare for Ireland. This whole situation had him wound tight. Kat on the brink of tears for that half-hour of waiting had done macramé on his intestines. Christ. Her little sighs had ripped open a part of his heart he'd thought had been walled off eons ago. Now, he couldn't stand not knowing what that matronly witch was telling her.

He still fumed that Kat accused him of having the morals of a weasel. He'd fought for over a decade to escape the compulsion to do another person's bidding just to get ahead. To be his own man, ruling his own kingdom. When he'd been undergoing Sentry training he'd probably have done anything Bryce and Quinn asked, but he had a moral line beyond which he'd never cross. He'd watched Grant Ryan cross that line several times to get a deal closed. And Kat dared suggest him that despicable?

The last place he wanted to be was here, stuck with Bryce, who'd been texting on his iPhone since the second he sat.

"When will you be leaving?" Matt asked, desperate to distract his brain.

Bryce held up his forefinger and went back to texting.

His pissed off soared into dangerous waters.

A few seconds later Bryce said, "Well, I sure as fuck won't be leaving without her. And she sure as hell won't be leaving without you." His phone chimed. He glanced at the message. "Damn it. We can't find one of the other Pleiads. Serenity's gone off the grid. That girl knows her ass has to be on its way to Ireland. This is a goddamned —"

"Clusterfuck?" Matt interrupted.

"You bet your ass it is. Here I thought I'd finally got all seven of those slippery women doing what they're supposed to and then…damn it. You have no idea how fucking frustrating they can be." Bryce slid his phone in his pocket and glared at Matt. "So, this thing with you and my daughter…"

"Maybe it's some wild chemistry, but it's not meant to be."

Bryce's eyebrows shot upward. "Are you buying into that wishful-thinking bullcrap?"

Matt shrugged. God he hated Bryce's tone, which reduced him to a cornered teenager with his father about to give him a grow-up-and-get-real chat.

Bryce slumped down on the sofa and ran a hand through his hair. After a long sigh he said, "She's all that I've got left of Lynn. Her whole life was stolen from me. Birthdays, learning to drive, graduating from school, first dates…the whole thing. Now she's confused about this business and lost, although I've no doubt Char is in there setting her straight and God knows what else. I shudder to imagine what she's telling her about us. I'm not ready to take that mental step from my-ten year-old to a thirty-year-old that's shacking up with *you*."

"But you'd be okay with her and Jason getting it on?"

Bryce scowled. "I'm not okay with her and *anyone*."

"You could control Jason, though. I could see how that might look good from your perspective. But the wuss couldn't defend himself against a Chihuahua. Acquisitions would roast his ass if he was against a fence, even if he does have some sort of telekinesis ability."

Bryce swore. He rolled his eyes upward. "I was desperate to get her here. Jason's story…I had hoped he was the one. But not because I thought him strong enough to protect her, or even worthy of her. I could train him. I just wanted her here."

Matt sighed. The two of them sat in silence. Unable to focus on anything other than his fury at Bryce, he scooted forward on his chair. "I would've happily died trying to help Quinn."

Bryce's eyelids drifted closed and he blew out a long exhale. "Yes, you would've. I have no doubt. But that wasn't what he wanted. We're not doing this again, Matt. It's in the past. Arguing won't get us anywhere right now. Someday, you might have a child and you will understand."

"Don't patronize me."

"Get over it. You must go to Ireland if we expect Katherine to go willingly." He pointed a finger at Matt. "Now don't be thinking I'm anywhere near okay with you and she being together. That's just…damn." He trailed off, running a hand over his face.

"It's Kat. She goes by Kat. She will go with you."

Bryce shielded his face with his hand and shook his head. He whipped his hand away. "You just don't get it yet, do you? If you and she are really destined, then you have to be together for this thing in Ireland."

"There's no proof on us being destined."

"Here I thought *I* was having issues accepting this." He rolled his eyes and looked heavenward. "Do the gods need to strike you over the head to get this? You've been bouncing into each other's lives for a very long time. You marked her. She dimension hopped with you. Twice. That in itself is a miracle, but apparently with a destined it's easier. If you are bound to be together…if you've bonded and you desert her, or God forbid, you die doing something stupid, then she will want to follow you into whatever level of afterlife you've earned. That's how it works. But she can't be departing this life. Not yet. You know what kind of hell will be unleashed if she or her daughter is missing when the veil lowers on Samhain? For once you need to do what's right. Move beyond your shit with me."

He hated that Bryce might be right. "Who was your source that said she might bump into me at some point?"

"What?" Bryce's face scrunched up in confusion.

"You said you had a source when you cornered me at that benefit the other day."

Bryce pinched the bridge of his nose. "Quinn. When he was dying he said you were the key to her being in this dimension."

"How did he know that?"

"I've got no clue. Did you and he have a chat about one of her jumps or something?"

His chest clamped tight and he fell back into the chair.

"I'll be damned. I never put it together about her being here, or jumping here that is, but Quinn must've."

"What happened?"

"That first time she appeared in my life she materialized right in front of me as if out of thin air. She was wet and half dead. She passed out almost immediately. I freaked and called Quinn, figuring he could fix her if she was hurt."

Bryce cursed softly. "He never said anything to me. Did he heal her?"

"Yes. And then she disappeared, but Quinn told me she'd gone home. And that I shouldn't worry. I didn't think that she'd really and truly disappeared to her other dimension. I'd assumed he figured out where she belonged and took her home."

"That's another reason Quinn knew you needed to survive on that god-awful day he died. He suspected you and she were…connected. He was as committed to the vow of Pleiades' protection as any of us."

"I know." He could accept that as a reason Quinn requested Bryce drag him away and not allow him to burn what he could of his healing power to heal him. He understood Quinn's soul-deep commitment to the Pleiades.

Bryce worked his jaw back-and-forth for a few seconds and then produced an annoying half smile. "You know, Matt, for someone so against us druids, you've acquired quite a few fans. Eli is an arrogant ass toward most of us, but defends you at every turn. I know he's hiding something about what happened during that car-chase fiasco. I tried to get it out of him three times, but the fucker's tight-lipped. Yeah, I know you two don't hate each other. That boy would do anything for you, guilt aside over him having the better childhood. So, you might fight this, but when you choose to walk this path, you've got friends who have your back."

Matt reluctantly nodded.

Chapter Twenty-One

Kat's heart relocated to her gut when Matt stomped past her on his way to Eli's SUV. So much for the possibility of apologizing. She scooted into the passenger seat of the other SUV, next to her father. No one else got in. A solo ride with her father. *Great.*

"Hey," Bryce tossed her way.

"Is Matt coming with us to Ireland?" She refused to get on a plane without him.

"I'll make sure he does."

Crap. Forcing him to accompany her on this trip would probably escalate his resentment toward her.

Bryce pinched his nose, ran a hand through his dark hair and then blew out a long exhale. This was not the fierce leader she'd seen inside. Softly he said, "I don't want to fight you. I'm sorry about everything in there. I just…" He leveled his gaze on her. "I lost you so long ago."

"Yeah." She pointed at the road where the taillights of the other SUV bobbed in the distance. "You better get going."

He cranked the car and put it in drive. The car jerked

forward, slamming her against the seat. She rushed to buckle the seat belt.

After an interminable period of silence and tricky driving on icy roads, she rested her head on the headrest. "We're going to have to talk about it. Me and Matt."

"He and you..." His knuckles lost their color as he gripped the wheel tight. "Did he tell you about the past? About Quinn and walking away from us?"

"Some of it. Sounded like a tough situation."

"Quinn was my best friend, my right hand. He'd been... shit, the things the OLM did to him was something no son should ever see. Matt went a little crazy. If I thought Matt could've saved him, I would've let him do anything he could, but he was too inexperienced. I did what I had to in order to get him out of there." Bryce drove in silence for a while and then lowered his voice to the point Kat had to strain to hear him. "I probably would've done the same thing Matt did if I was in his shoes. Walk away from us, I mean."

"I'm sorry you both lost Quinn, but I'm glad you forced Matt to leave."

"Does he love you?" Bryce asked.

"I don't know." She ran a hand over her hair to smooth it away from her face, even though it was already in place. Her heart beat so hard that her chest hurt. "Maybe we shouldn't talk about this."

"But you love him."

She nodded, swiping at a few stray tears.

"Shit. Please don't cry. It'll only make me madder at him."

"Matt and I had a fight in the middle of all that drama back at his house. A misunderstanding, really. But now I don't know where we stand. You might just get your wish that we will split up." Somehow she felt safe telling her father this, even though she knew she shouldn't. Matt would hate this. But her mind reminded her that he'd left her alone with her father for this drive.

"I'm sorry about what I said. I just want you to be with the right druid. One that can give you what you deserve. I don't doubt the boy could protect you, but look at what he's already done to you. You're a goddamned mess."

Laughter bubbled up in her. "Charlotte was right. You are just like him. The two of you are stubborn. And controlling."

"Charlotte…" He shook his head. "She's a scheming old broad."

"I screwed it up this time, not him. I said the wrong thing and I don't know if he'll forgive me. Just promise me you won't kill him. Can you also, please, release him from whatever you're holding over him?"

He granted her a weak smile. "All right. But if he wants to be my son-in-law, he's going to have to earn it."

She smiled. Hope blossomed in her chest at the prospect of finally knowing her real father.

He looked over at her. The Scottish accent thickened. "You're the spitting image of your mother, you know. She'd have been so proud of you."

"What happened to her? We went to the zoo—"

"The zoo…damn it. That was all my fault. I'd told her for three weeks we'd do the zoo the next day, and finally she got pissed and did it herself. You redheads and your temper, no offense."

"We were on our way to see the giraffes and then there were these guys. One of them shot her with a dart. That's about all I remember."

"She jumped you to your alternate and dumped you before she jumped back. They took her to a facility in Europe. Before we could get to her, they shot her. With a gun. Quinn was with me when we found her…" His voice cracked and he cleared his throat. "She was too far gone for him to help her." His reddened gaze turned to meet hers. "She loved you so much. I wanted to follow her into the afterlife, but she asked me to stay until you came back." He maneuvered the car into a hangar at the airport.

She swallowed the lump in her throat.

Bryce blinked his eyes a few times. "She wanted you to know how sorry she was that she couldn't help you understand everything."

She nodded, too choked up to speak.

He parked the car and turned toward her. "She'd want you to have this. It belongs to the descendant in her line." He removed a small ring from a chain around his neck. "It's a toe ring."

Her entire hand tingled when she took the ring. It had a depiction of what she suspected was a constellation on its top. Probably Pleiades. "Thank you."

"I'm here for you, if you need me," he said gruffly.

She blinked against the moisture in her eyes. She unclicked her belt and lunged toward him, enveloping him in a hug. His strong arms locked her against him.

He whispered, "I'm sorry."

She pulled out of his embrace. "I think we've got a plane to catch. Can you please try to get along with Matt on this flight?"

"We'll see."

• • •

If Kat had been a nail biter, then at least she'd have an outlet for the anxiety of being stuck in this private jet with too many people focused on her. No one talked, and she had nothing to do. Someone could've at least loaned her a magazine.

She should sleep since it was the middle of the night. But with Mr. Hotness seated directly across from her, texting nonstop and throwing brief, indecipherable glances her way, sleep was the last thing on her mind. His data plan must be amazing. What she wouldn't give to have internet access. A little web surfing might help pass the time.

Her father darted a glance her way, glowered at Matt, and then went back to texting, Facebooking or whatever on his iPhone. Four guard-like druids toward the back of the plane stared at her between interest in portable electronics. Their thoughts were a jumble of protective duty and icky sex fantasy. No other Pleiades on board, though. She could've used a little girl support. Charlotte told her Bryce had mandated a decade ago that the Pleiades were not allowed to travel together. Something about air attacks that didn't sound reassuring.

She'd pretended sleep for about an hour to avoid staring at Matt, not that it worked. Her body lit up every time his hot gaze slid her way, however rare that was.

As exhaustion pushed to the forefront of her mind, she gave up on avoidance of what she wanted to stare at most. Her gaze dragged over the muscular planes of Matt's body, covered by a long-sleeved, dark T-shirt. She drank him in as she scanned down the strong cut of his thighs in those jeans. Oh God. He was turned on. Her gaze snapped to his face. Crap, he wasn't texting anymore.

His eyebrows hitched upward. An unreadable expression passed over his face. He looked gorgeous, but he didn't look happy. Regret lodged itself deep in her stomach.

"So, Kat, did Charlotte get you up to date on what's about to happen in Ireland?" Bryce asked from a few seats over and across.

Her cheeks blazed. How mortifying to have her father catch her doing a body scan. "Sure." *Not really.*

Bryce nodded. "Great. I just want you to be ready."

"Can you rescind whatever threat you put out on Matt's sister?" she requested.

Bryce raised his eyebrows. "Okay." Softly he added, "I'd

never intended to follow through. His sister is, uh, delicate."

"Thanks. It'd be great if we can all call a truce for a little bit. This…." She gestured with her hands to everything around her. "This is overwhelming enough. The minefield the two of you planted is too much for me to negotiate right now."

"All right." Bryce's gaze moved to Matt.

He ignored Bryce and met her stare. Did he feel trapped? Resentful? His expression conveyed a whole lot of latent anger.

He asked Bryce, "How long are you planning to keep me hostage? I've got a business about to implode without me." He glanced down at his phone.

"Let's just get through the bloody weekend. I'm sure they can do without you for a few days. Then you can get back to your life."

Clearly, Matt didn't want to be here. And didn't want her. Dragging in a hard breath, she looked away, struggling not to cry. She didn't want to do this world without him. She should go home, but she'd promised Charlotte she'd do whatever it was she had to do in Ireland. Trapped.

She asked her numb legs to stand, and stumbled toward the bathroom, desperate to get away from all the too-curious gazes. As she pushed into the small stainless-steel room she swiped angrily at a few renegade tears. The pain in her chest pressed like a twisting blade.

The bathroom door clicked behind her. She'd been followed.

• • •

Matt heard the catch in her voice and knew she suppressed tears. He'd never felt another person's emotions like he did hers. Her misery twisted something deep in his gut with a need to soothe and protect her.

"Kat," he said gruffly. He reached for her shoulders and pulled her to face him. And drew her into his body. "You're killing me."

She broke into sobs and clung to him.

He wrapped her tight. Yet somehow it wasn't enough. He wanted to lock her to him, tight enough that neither one of them could escape. He slid his hand up her arm until he reached the back of her neck and cupped her head.

She swept a hand across her face, removing some runaway tears. Her glassy, reddened gaze met his, so filled with pain. He understood that pain. It burned him alive with a want so intense that it panicked him.

"Living in that other world, I always sensed there was something going on, something important, but I wasn't sure what it was. It was as if I knew those weird world shifts meant something. That they weren't just random. I sensed something was very wrong about my life. It nearly drove me mad."

"Mmm-hmm," he mumbled, wondering where this was headed.

"I think that, and then us, is why my head's so messed up right now. I'm not sure who to trust. I'm terrified I don't have enough control over the world-shifting thing to stay here or go there. I'm scared to read another's thoughts because I might get overwhelmed like what happened at that benefit. I don't want to go home because the career that I built as a vet has fallen apart due to my absences. Crap, I'm sorry I'm rambling. You don't need to listen. I know you don't want to be here."

He kept her snug against his chest. "I'm here."

"I'm sorry for what I said. I didn't mean how that came out back at your house."

"Yeah." He was sorry he'd gone off the deep end, but she'd hit a sore spot.

"I know you didn't mean to hurt me either." This was said with a lift at the end, the words more of a question than a statement.

"I didn't," he said and glanced down. Her lips parted on a ragged inhale. He brushed a finger down her cheek. God, he wanted this woman on every level with a distracting attraction that made it hard for him to keep his mind on talking.

She pushed her chest away from him to make eye contact. "Do you even want to be here? With me and doing this?"

He followed the chain of his dog tags to where it disappeared between her breasts. He liked them there. Perfect. "I've never said I didn't want to be with you. The me-and-you part of all of this I've always wanted. I want to give us a chance, but I hate the fact there's some sort of higher power driving us together. I've always lived by making my own way in the world and being in charge of my own decisions. This is way out of our control. I don't like that. The being here that has to do with druid crap...well, I've got to come to terms with that."

She nodded and moistened her lips.

"You're flushed." He trailed his finger over to her soft lips. "Are you thinking about kissing?"

She gasped out, "Yes." She cupped his cheek. "I really am sorry I hurt you. I didn't want you being with me to be about you and my father."

"There's only the two of us."

Her tongue darted out to moisten her lips. "Kiss me."

His lips met hers, flicking over her lower lip until she opened her mouth. He circled his tongue slowly in her mouth as his hands moved down over her body. She trembled and fell into him, moaning.

"Not here," she whispered.

"Why not? They can speculate out there, but no one here has X-ray vision or super-hearing ability."

"My father is out there, along with a few extremely horny druids."

"Horny? If the fuckers even think anything with you, you tell me and I'll gut 'em."

She giggled. "Even your mean talk is sexy."

He grinned. "There's no time, anyway. I just heard the landing gear drop." How he wanted a few hours…hell, a lifetime…with her, and no druids within a thousand miles.

Her hand cupped his cheeks and an impish smile curved her lips. "Later, then."

"Yeah," he croaked out.

Chapter Twenty-Two

The light of dawn outside the window of the SUV tickled the horizon, which threw her internal clock into a free fall. In her world it was the middle of the night, but in Ireland the breakfast sausages would be frying. All she wanted was to slip beneath the sheets of her bed for about a day. Maybe a week. At this point any bed would do, preferably somewhere private and safe. And with Matt in it.

She wasn't sure who or what they waited for here at the airport. But they'd been idling for five minutes in this SUV.

"I could do with a huge black coffee. I'm sure there's somewhere in Belfast that offers a crack of dawn cup," Bryce announced from the driver's seat. He checked his watch and mumbled, "Wish the boys would hurry up with their report on the safety of our travel path."

"I'll take a double shot of anything caffeinated," Matt grumbled.

Unexpectedly, a fourth passenger slid into the rear seat next to her.

The newcomer smoothed her shoulder-length black hair

with interwoven red highlights. Pale blue eyes met hers. "I'm Serenity," She met the questioning gaze of both men in the front seats and snorted out a laugh. "I just had this weird image of being at an AA meeting. My name's Serenity and I'm a Pleiades."

"If only it was a problem as easy to kick as alcoholism," Kat muttered. She smiled and held out her hand. "I'm Kat."

Serenity shook her hand. "Amen to that, sister. I knew if Matt liked you, then you'd be cool." She smiled.

Bryce interrupted. "Where the bloody hell have you been and what are you doing here? You know we don't travel like this. Too much risk to be out in the open with you guys together."

Serenity rolled her eyes. "God, you can be such an ass. What happened to: *Hey Serenity. How're you doing?*"

Bryce expelled an agitated sigh.

Serenity rolled her eyes. "I'm here to help. Got some info for you."

"Fine. I'm sorry. What were you doing to be of *help*?" Bryce grumbled, clearly trying his best to rid his face of the what-the-hell storm cloud.

"That apology sucked, old man." Serenity crossed her arms and slumped in the seat.

"For fuck's sake, Serenity, spit it out." Bryce cranked around to glare.

Serenity sighed and glanced disparagingly at Kat. "He's really got such a potty mouth, doesn't he? I swear he drops the F-bomb almost every other sentence."

She laughed. "Got him pegged on that one."

"I remember Auntie Lynn complaining about it a lot. Since she's not been around, he's only gotten worse." She made a sad face. "It's such a shame you didn't get to know your mother well. She was one entertaining lady."

Bryce cleared his throat. "We are not doing a memorylane stroll right now."

Serenity explained, "I'm sort of like the black sheep of the Pleiades, Kat. I don't obey the rules, at least the security ones."

Bryce muttered under his breath. His phoned dinged. One scan of the incoming message and he pulled the SUV away from the airport hangar. "Serenity…details. Now."

Serenity said, "Fine. I got intel that Acquisitions is here. I've been doing a little recon in downtown Belfast— "

"How can I possibly keep you safe when you insist on doing stupid ass shit like that?" Bryce asked.

Matt chuckled. "She can take care of herself. The girl's well trained. Don't forget she's ex-MI6."

"It's my job to see to her safety," Bryce said.

"I can be *invisible*. So, I'm probably safer than anyone else you could send in. The area is crawling with Acquisitions. It's like they're pinging radar off everything, but don't know exactly what they're looking for. How did they know we were here? You think their Sighter can predict more than just dimension jumps?"

"No clue," said Bryce.

"Where exactly are we going? Long drive?" Kat asked.

"About an hour south of Belfast. I guess we're skipping coffee and doing a quick drive through town," Bryce announced.

"How're you holding up with all this, Matt?" Serenity asked as she laid a hand on his shoulder.

"Fine," he answered in a clipped tone.

"That good, huh?" Serenity got comfortable in the seat and pulled out her cell phone, scrolling through a few incoming messages. "I'm glad you're here, Matt."

Jealousy hit her hard. Did he and this girl have something going on?

Serenity patted her arm and whispered, "He's all yours.

We've been friends a long time. Trust me when I say there's nothing other than friendship there."

As they merged into early morning traffic, Bryce announced, "We're being followed and they're getting aggressive behind us."

He cut a sharp right and then left, the wheels screeching complaint. "They're still there."

"Drop Kat and I at the next corner immediately after you turn. If you're fast on the turn, they won't see us because of the large building," Serenity ordered.

"No," Bryce said.

"You two can lead them on a merry chase. Take 'em out and whatever. We'll meet you at the train station in an hour."

"No," Bryce said again.

"Matt…" Serenity pleaded.

"She can hold her own." He turned to glare at Serenity. "You swear on whatever you hold sacred that you can do this and you will get her back to me in one piece?"

"You betcha." She checked and chambered a round in both of her handguns. "Besides, Char always said we're stronger when together. Bryce just doesn't believe it. We can dimension hop if we get into trouble."

Matt's eyes narrowed and he said softly, "No matter *who* or what you run into, Serenity, you'll make it?"

"We will make it," Serenity promised.

Bryce floored it and cornered a tight right. He hit the brakes, but before the car came to a pseudo-stop, Serenity pulled Kat out of the car. They jumped over a snowbank, and Kat struggled not to skid right into the building on the icy sidewalk.

After running and sliding on icy patches through several back alleys, Serenity held a single finger against her lips and indicated for her to follow her through a restaurant. The smell of coffee and pastry might've tempted her stomach, if she could just catch her breath. Jealously she noted Serenity's chest barely moved. Dancing kept her in shape, but it wasn't as if she did track sprints on a daily basis.

They skirted out the back door into another alley. And into the corner turn.

"Don't move," ordered an unfamiliar man.

Serenity froze as the muzzle of a gun lay, almost casually, against her forehead. She held her hands up, allowing her gun to fall. A tall man with insane cheekbones slammed Serenity into the brick building so hard that Kat heard Serenity's teeth crunch. His fist encircled Serenity's throat to hold her in place.

"Let her go," Kat ordered, infusing every bit of mind persuasion she had.

The man's glacial green eyes glided to her. A chill slid over her skin with the impression of death. Instinct pushed her to bolt from him and the danger he promised.

He said low with the hint of a Eastern European accent, "Your skills won't work on me." With his free hand he removed a small device from his pocket. Kat screamed as her world went electric. Jolts of energy sent her tumbling to the cold ground, muscles twitching. The bastard tased her! Once her world stopped spasming, she tried to get into the man's mind, but received no thoughts. All she picked up from him was self-assurance and control.

Serenity's leg kicked upward, scoring a glancing nut crunch. He backed up a step with a grunt, his fingers on her throat loosening. She tore out of his grip.

He snatched Serenity's wrist as she turned. One of her ankles twisted inside his and she almost caused him to lose balance. With a graceful twist she put several feet between them. She crouched and stared at him, her breathing heavy. "Let us go. We are no threat to you."

"You and all of *them* threaten the world, according to the OLM."

"Now you believe that bullshit? I never thought you a narrow-minded prick like them. We plan to save the world tonight." She reached down for Kat, helping her to a wobbly stand. "We're leaving now."

"The hell you are. What are you doing out here?" His lips shifted into a scowl as he whipped a gun from his belt.

"Will you shoot me, Alexi?" She backed away from him, blocking Kat with her body.

Kat heard the *pfft* of his suppressed gun firing. Serenity jumped backward, pushing Kat into the wall.

"Are you shot?" Kat asked, a note of hysteria in her tone.

"No," Serenity said dully. They turned to see a man lying on the sidewalk, a small bullet hole center of his forehead. He was dressed in standard Acquisitions black tactical. When Kat looked for Alexi, he was gone.

"Did he miss?" Kat asked softly.

"Alexi Jovec doesn't miss." Serenity rubbed her throat.

"Who was that?"

"Right now, Alexi is moonlighting with the OLM's Acquisitions department, but I don't get why the deadliest assassin on the planet is messing around with them. Or why the hell Alexi just shot one of the Acquisition guys and not me or you, when clearly his mission is to get us."

"You know him, don't you?"

"He's..." Serenity massaged her forehead.

Kat understood that state of confused uncertainty only too well. Serenity and that terrifying killer had history, and weren't over. She granted Serenity a half-smile. "I thought *my* love life was messed up."

"Something happened between us and it was... memorable. But it's a dead end. So beyond over. How about we keep this little incident between us. This will give Bryce a coronary."

"We're almost sisters. So, your secret's safe here. I don't

like that guy, and not just because he tased me."

"No one likes him. He only hit you with a light shock. Had he cranked it, you'd be immobile for an hour."

"That somehow makes it okay? I can't believe you're actually defending him. He just tased me!"

"Shit." Serenity pinched her nose. "I'm sorry. He is an ass most of the time." Serenity glanced her over as if to ensure she was okay. She announced, "To the train station."

Chapter Twenty-Three

"Braless in a white nightgown? What the hell? This is not my thing," Serenity announced as she plucked at the front of the simple white cotton dress.

Kat squirmed in the thin dress that had been thrown her way, wondering if their plan was to freeze on their way to whatever outdoor gala Charlotte planned. Kat had worn three layers when they entered the remote cottage estate not long ago, and feared frostbite in the biting winds and snow. A rush intro of the other Pleiades women minutes before they did a communal strip and donned these gowns remained a blur of names and faces. Yet she felt comforted by their presence.

"Hair down, ladies. It's custom. Serenity, suck it up and deal," Charlotte ordered.

Serenity waggled her middle finger at Charlotte's back. The teenager named Nicole giggled and threw Serenity a *you're-my-hero* smile.

Charlotte held open the door with a silent time-to-leave directive.

"Wait," Kat said, "If we're about to do some weird stone-circle druid ritual that involves sacrificing someone, or blood, then I'm out."

Charlotte rolled her eyes. "Sweetie, we are not druids. Besides, that business was only done by an extremist druid sect led by a drug addict who thought himself a precog, but the man couldn't predict that his dog would shit after a meal."

"You know that because you were alive in the 1600s?" Serenity asked.

"If I didn't think you could kick my ass in hand to hand, I'd smack you for that," Charlotte said, "An ancestor kept a really interesting journal."

Serenity whispered to Kat on their way out the front door, "The old broad said we had to go completely naked but there's no way in hell I'm going unarmed." She raised the long white hem to reveal a thigh holster.

Kat smiled. She halted at the door, gazing at Matt. She didn't want to do this without him.

"You're with her," Bryce pointed at Matt.

She hugged herself against the draft from the open door.

"Why aren't you coming?" Matt asked Bryce as he walked toward her.

"Only the seven women and any destined are allowed out there by the rocks. I've seen it once. They need you guys for protection since they might get a little wrapped up in what they're doing."

Matt asked, "Why not send the best you've got to protect them?"

"Only a bonded druid can take what they're about to do without going a bit…uh, wild."

"What does that mean?"

"You'll see."

"What about you and the others?"

"We'll cover the perimeter. This is what we're good at." Bryce tapped his wireless ear communicator and listened. He ordered, "Report Red team." He glanced back at Matt. "Go. You do your thing with her and them. That's your job now." Bryce yanked out his cell, dismissing him.

Matt took Kat's hand.

She said, "I'm so cold." She shuddered as an arctic blast of wind tore through the thin gown.

He wrapped his arm around her. As they crested the hill at a fast jog, the freezing dissipated into a perfect seventy-something. "Well that's weird," she mumbled.

"Everything about this will probably be weird," he replied and pointed toward the women. "Go. I'll wait out here on the periphery with Brian."

Charlotte approached a gigantic irregular bolder in a clearing and said, "Let's sing, ladies. For you newbies, you should recognize the tunes." She started a beautiful lullaby that Kat remembered. Her mother had sung it countless times. Its melody compelled. She sang.

When the song ended Charlotte laughed. "Now we dance." She started a new song.

Kat recognized this new song and recalled dancing with her mother. She laughed and joined into the fun of gyrating to the rhythm. She caught Matt's wide-eyed gaze and smiled. He fell back against a tree and ran a hand over his forehead. Concerned, she trotted over to him.

"What's wrong?" she asked.

"You ladies wove some sort of spell." He waved a hand toward Charlotte's husband, who rested his hands on his knees, breathing hard, and another guy who held onto a tree as if it was a lifeline with a fixed gaze on a twentysomething blonde whose name she didn't remember.

"What kind of spell? Are you hurt?" She reached out to touch him.

He backed up. "Don't. You put one finger on me right now and…holy hell, Kat. I'm hanging onto my sanity by a thread. I'll have you up against this tree and be inside you in about one second."

The air rushed out of her throat ending in an, "Oh." Then she cocked her head. She liked holding this much sexual power over him. "That doesn't sound so bad." She reached a finger out to touch him.

He stepped backward, avoiding her finger, and swallowed convulsively. "Please, go. Do whatever has to be done." He ran a hand through his hair. "Get over there. The compulsion… the drive is getting stronger, wildcat."

"Afterward, then?" She scanned his body slowly with a grin, enjoying his sharp intake of breath.

"You're going to kill me." He wrapped his fist around a tree branch.

The singing beckoned to her. Trancelike, she resumed the dance, which stopped when a deep blue glow developed in the center of the clearing.

The glowing mist parted and a humanlike form materialized at the periphery.

Her mother.

Charlotte said softly, "Each of us gets a moment with an ancestor. You get to go first tonight, Katherine." The six other women backed away.

Kat slowly walked toward the glowing mist, transfixed on the almost solid form of her long-dead mother. The form flipped her flowing strawberry-blonde hair over a shoulder and smiled reassuringly.

When she was within a few feet the shimmering image of her mother spoke. "Hi Katie-kat."

"Who are you?"

"That's complicated. Let's just say I'm the ghost of your mother. Yet I am all the descendants. We are one on this day of communication."

"Are you doing okay over there?"

The image of her mother smiled. "You seem to be acclimating to your new life."

"It's been a bit overwhelming."

"I am sorry I dumped you with that family. I did my best on short notice. But now, I need for you to give a message to Bryce."

Kat nodded.

"Tell him I am waiting. It is very important you tell him *it is time*. He can let go. His successor has arrived, and I am ready for him to join me."

Tears moistened Kat's cheeks, which she swiped away. "But I just got here. I don't even know him yet."

"I know, Katie-kat. It is not fair. But he has done all that was required of him."

"Right. I'll tell him."

"That's my girl. Now stop fighting what is right. Revel in your abilities. They will not go away. You must accept them, learn them and enjoy. How well I know that life is too short. Now go and claim that man over there as yours."

Kat eyed his tense form. "I don't know if he wants me, or all this."

The phantom laughed. "Dense males. It is time for you to make this happen. Follow your instincts." She shimmered into nothing. Gone.

Kat backed away from the shimmering doorway. In a daze she watched each of the other seven speak with their own personal phantom. She expected fireworks or an energy explosion or something when it was done, but the moment the last of the seven spoke with her ghost, the shimmering doorway disappeared—anticlimactic for something that could result in a universe-altering ending, if one of them no-showed.

A dull *pop-pop-pop* shattered the sudden silence.

"Everyone down. Get into the depression in the rock," Serenity ordered. "Someone's shooting from the other side of the rock. Move. Now!"

Kat dove into the shallow alcove in the massive rock structure beside Nicole and gazed at Matt, now a hundred yards away. He melted into the shadows of the forest behind him. *Oh God, don't let him die.*

Serenity unholstered her gun from her thigh. "Sorry if I flashed anyone." She cocked an eyebrow at Charlotte, daring her to comment. "The shooters are probably OLM Acquisition assholes. Isn't it Bryce's job to do perimeter guarding? I can't believe we're out here like sitting ducks with no protection."

Another volley of gunfire had rock pieces spewing around them.

"Shouldn't we pop away to our alternates?" asked Nicole.

Charlotte said. "We can't. We used too much magic for the Confirmation. We probably can't transition to our other dimensions for at least a day, or use our gifts very well for a while. It's the perfect time to ambush us." Charlotte glanced around. "Jen, can you cast a protective spell over us?"

A brunette shook her head. "Already tried. I'm tapped out."

Gunfire echoed from the area in the forest where the boys used to be.

Serenity announced, "Char, I think your husband got whoever is near them. I know Brian had a gun. Doesn't matter, though. We're all fucked. You hear that?"

Another volley of gunfire came from the other side of the rock.

Serenity said, "That's rifle fire. All we've got is my handgun and Brian's. That's a max of thirty rounds minus however many he uses to get the guys near them. They've got rifles and probably endless rounds. They'll pick us off, if we move."

"What's a round?" Jen asked.

"Seriously?" Serenity said. "A round is a bullet. I think this should be a lesson to us that we've got to stop staying apart. We need to train for this kind of disaster."

"I'll second that," Nicole said. She giggled. "You're pretty kickass, Serenity."

Serenity scowled. "There's nothing funny about this." She leaned around the rock depression to her right and shot twice.

Nicole said, "I'm pretty sure we get through this."

"You have a vision?" Charlotte asked.

Nicole leaned back with a tranquil smile.

Kat watched a shadow appear at the edge of the forest where Serenity had targeted. She pointed, and Serenity's gaze snapped to the shadow. The guy's hands were in the air in a clear what-the-hell signal. Kat recognized those high cheekbones, but didn't understand his gesture. "What was that about?" she whispered to Serenity. No one other than she and Serenity seemed to have noticed him.

"Shit, I almost shot him. He's…I think he will help us, which is good for us. Confusing as hell." Serenity mumbled. She mouthed to Alexi, "Sorry." The guy pointed to the opposite side of the forest with a clear *shoot-that-way*. Then disappeared. Serenity whirled and emptied five rounds to the left.

Kat's ears rang from the noise.

Serenity fell to a sit next to her. "I'm empty. No more bullets."

Kat whispered to her, "You think he will…help?"

Serenity shrugged. "He plays for his own team most of the time. I don't understand him."

A few more shots rang out and then nothing. They sat in silence for several tense minutes.

"Everyone okay?" Charlotte asked.

A round of yeses confirmed the all-around okay. The guys reappeared at the edge of the clearing and jogged to them.

Matt announced, "It's over. I don't know how, but they're all dead."

"Let's get out of here before more decide to show up. Everyone inside," Charlotte announced.

Everyone followed Charlotte, but Kat caught Serenity's arm as she stood. She whispered, "Was that really him again?"

Serenity nodded. Emotion clouded her face, and then she shook her head. "I don't get him. I think he helped us, but I don't know why. Forget it. Let's get inside."

For the first time Kat really looked at Matt. Relief that he was alive paralyzed her. There was an angry scrape along his left cheek and numerous tears in his shirt. "Oh God, what happened?" She touched his cheek with gentle fingers.

"I'll heal." His arms closed around her and he dragged her into his chest. He was so powerful, and right now she needed an anchor to hang onto. She knew she was safe with him.

He said, "It's time to get out of here."

Her vision blurred. She barely heard him say, "Trust me," before she was in his arms and he was running. She circled her arms around his neck and buried her face in his neck. Tears fell, and she couldn't tell if she was crying from happiness, relief or fear. When they neared the cottage, she brushed away the moisture from her face.

"Stop," she said. "Please."

He halted.

"Put me down." He let her slide to the ground, supporting her until she had her balance. She stared up into his too handsome face. There would never be another man for her. There never had been. "I need truth between us. Tell me there might be another person in this world for you and I will walk away. We can end this. Otherwise, I want this to be forever. I'm not into sharing."

Hoarsely he said, "Only you."

She rubbed circular motions over his chest. "I love you, Matt. And this belongs to me."

He swiftly inhaled. "What'd you do? It burns." He unbuttoned his shirt and stretched it away from the left side of his chest. A red *meandros* symbol rested above his heart.

She recognized it as the Greek symbol for unity and eternity.

She stared up at him, blinking. She hadn't expected that. "I didn't mean to do that. I mean, I want it, but, crap. If you don't want it, maybe I can take it back."

He pulled her into his arms. "Leave it alone. It just surprised me, but it stays."

Her chest clenched. "Really?"

"Yes." The sincerity of that one word reflected in his expression.

She threw her arms around his neck and buried her face in his chest.

"Please tell me you're not crying again, Kat. Shit, you are crying. What did I do now?"

"It's the good kind of crying." Her voice was muffled against his chest. "This is a lot to take in. I just saw my dead mother as a phantom goddess. Then there's my father, you, me being Pleiades, us almost getting shot…"

"One thing at a time. We'll figure it out."

"Together?"

He nodded. "The temperature is dropping out here. Whatever magic made it tolerable is dissipating. Time to go inside."

"I have a message for my father from the phantom thing that I think was my mother. I can't believe I talked to her. She was so beautiful. Just like I remember her." Those few moments with her mother gave her peace. Her mom was okay in her afterlife and waited for her father.

He gripped her hand and fast walked for the cottage. The smell of apple cider powered up her nose as they pushed inside.

Bryce stalked toward them. "You all right? I just heard what happened."

"Where the hell were you and your guys?"

"Fighting a bloody war at the south end of the property."

"Did one of your guys make it to the area near us and

take out some hostiles?"

Bryce shook his head. "No."

"Then, I'm not sure what happened or how we got out of there. We were out of ammo, they had rifles, and, yet, the Acquisitions team was miraculously snipered."

Bryce clapped him on the shoulder. "Welcome back to the world of the weird. These things happen. The OLM is still out there. They just backed off a bit. I've got men on the perimeter. But everyone needs to be alert. We've got to protect all the ladies." He grinned and handed Kat a baggy fleece pullover. Softly he asked, "Aside from the afterward excitement how'd it go?" Knowledge swirled in his gaze.

She pulled on the fleece, which fell to her knees. "Good. Weird. I saw Mom. She gave me a message for you."

Sadness passed through his eyes. "What'd she say?"

"She said *it is time* and a new successor has been chosen."

Bryce nodded.

She waited for him to clarify what that meant. Instead he held his hand out to Matt. "If you want to be my son-in-law, you're going to have to ask for her hand."

"I figured that." Matt returned his handclasp.

Bryce reached his left hand in to lock their hands together.

"What is it with you guys and burning me tonight?" He yanked his hand free of Bryce's and exposed the blue Sentry tattoo on his wrist. Above that rested a new mark, one that she recognized had been on Bryce's wrist.

"I thought so," Bryce said softly. He rotated his wrist into view to show that his leadership mark was gone.

"What is this?" Matt rubbed at the new sigil.

"You've been chosen, Son. This is way beyond you and me and our wants. You're in, and you're in charge." Bryce grinned. "Honestly, I can't tell you how relieved I am to pass the torch. These young kids are a handful."

"You're fucking with me, right?"

"You're the new druid leader?" She worried he'd bolt for the door.

Matt met the gazes of the thirty or so now silent druids and Pleiades surrounding them. To Bryce he said, "I'm not…I really don't have the time. Hell, I haven't even *been* a druid for so long that I'm not sure I'm the best qualified."

"The goddesses chose you," Bryce said. "It's hard for me to admit this but you are a good choice. Look at what you did for that shitter business, Ryan Corp. You took it from a barely surviving tech corporation to the most sought-after military contractor. Maybe you can get these witches to actually listen to you when it comes to their safety."

Charlotte snorted a few yards away.

Bryce scowled at her but said to Matt, "Yeah, good luck on that, but there's always hope."

Kat squeezed his arm. "Maybe this is your sign that you can back off at the corporation a bit. Delegate more? Maybe be chairman of the board but not CEO? Okay, based on that look, no. But my experience over the past few days indicates the druid side of your life will let you utilize those Ranger skills far more than sitting in an office with a picture of a blank sky." She frowned. "By the way, was that painting your choice? And if so, why?"

He laughed, leaned down, and kissed her. "The picture is supposed to be inspiring and relaxing."

"It's a blank sky. I don't get it. Maybe if it had a bird or a witch on a broom in it or something." She smiled in relief when he cracked a grin.

He glanced around at all the druids staring at them. "It would be my honor."

All in unison raised cups with a resounding, "Here. Here."

She whispered to Bryce, "Does that mean you're going to die?"

"We all depart this life at some point." He roped his arm

around her shoulders and pulled her into him. "Don't look so lost. I'm not going to give up the ghost yet. Matt will require quite a bit of work before I go."

She watched Matt give everyone he greeted his perfect smile. He said whatever was right and reassuring as he worked through the crowd, but she recognized the same stiff public persona she'd glimpsed at the benefit. Remote. Unreadable. This Matt scared her. No one else noticed.

Eli clapped him on the back and laughed an I-told-you-so. Charlotte scowled at Matt and then pulled him close to whisper something. Matt pinned Kat with an inscrutable gaze and massaged his forehead. She didn't understand that. He moved on to greet Serenity. And so it went for at least a half hour.

She followed him when he slipped out of the ruckus a while later into a dark formal dining room. He pulled out a dining chair to sit and massage his forehead.

"What's wrong?" she asked, moving in to massage his shoulders.

He continued his head rub, not even startled. He must've known she'd followed. "Headache."

"You sure you're okay with all this?" she asked.

His hand halted its head rub. "You're cute when you bite your lip." He snagged her and pulled her into his lap.

"You're not okay with this, are you?" She moved a few strands of hair off his forehead.

"Druids…being around so many magical people makes my head hurt. Always has."

"I'm sorry. Maybe I can help." She pressed her lips against his. When he kissed her back everything but them disappeared—the noise from the other room, the stress of what to do about her job, and the worry over his reaction to everything. The world narrowed to him and her, and the feel of his soft lips on hers. She moaned as their tongues touched. The ridge of his erection nudged between her legs.

She straddled him. The white gown rode above her knees. Need gathered low in her abdomen. She rubbed against him, relieved at the friction of his jeans against her naked skin.

He pulled back from the kiss, his eyes blazing with the wildness that drove her insane. It tempted her to push him harder. To see him lose control.

His large hand slid down her back to cup her butt. "You're...naked under this thing? Shit, if I'd know that outside...you're lucky I didn't know. We can't do this in here."

"But we are doing this." It wasn't a question.

"God, Kat." He swallowed hard. "Let me find out where we're staying tonight." He moved as if to rise.

She cupped his face, halting him. "You don't have to do all this alone anymore. I'm here. A few of those out there seem to truly like you. They believe in you."

"You read their thoughts or whatever?"

She nodded.

"Give me a minute." A few steps away he turned back. "Stay." He held up a single finger. "One minute. No popping away."

"Who knows how long I can wait..." She burst out laughing at the panicked expression on his face. "Hurry."

Minutes later he pulled her into a cottage a short distance from the main house. The moment the door closed, she gripped the edge of his shirt, yanked him down to her, and crushed her lips to his.

He released a muffled grunt into her mouth and tugged her body against his. Standing on tiptoes, she stretched up to wrap her arms around his neck, bringing them even closer. Their tongues tangled as he slid his hands around the back of her thighs. She could feel against her belly how much he wanted her, his heat burning through the thin gown. She wanted him, desperately, and whimpered into his mouth. He lifted her a little and thrust his pelvis against her.

She rasped, “Don’t stop.” She needed him to touch her. Everywhere.

“I’m only getting started.” With a growl he crushed her mouth to his, kissing so passionately that she felt branded. He carried her to the kitchen, placing her on the table. “Let me taste you.”

Kneeling down, he cupped her ass with his hands and let his tongue swirl between her folds, focusing on the tiny nub at the top. A tremor racked her body and she moaned, arching into him.

He smiled and continued his torture, licking, swirling. Seconds later she let out a low moan and clawed at his shoulders. “Please…”

“Not yet, baby.”

Her fingers speared through his hair and halted as if she couldn’t decide if she wanted to force him up or pin him in his spot.

“Oh God.” She moaned, and rocked against his mouth.

“You want me inside?” he asked.

She nodded.

He slid one finger into her heat. She clenched around him and moaned. He slowly pulled out and added another finger.

Her hips arched to meet his fingers. “Just a bit more, wildcat.” He leaned in and flicked his tongue across her clit. She tensed and clenched tighter around his fingers. Then her tremors began. “I love watching you come.”

“Please. I need you, Matt. *Now.*” She unzipped him and wrapped her hand around his straining length.

“Kat…” He groaned, closing his eyes.

“Hurry.” She slid her hand up and down, delighting in his tremor.

He slipped his hands under her ass and surged into her in one powerful stroke. His head fell back on a moan. He gripped her hips and held her in place as he moved.

"Oh God, Matt..." She angled her pelvis upward to meet him. "Faster."

"I can't hold on, wildcat."

He pumped his hips until she felt her world shatter. A few thrusts later he groaned his release. "That was so fucking—"

"Perfect," she completed the thought. "But we've got to be careful in the future. I can't take the pill."

He smoothed hair away from her face. "I'd be okay, if you..."

"Really?"

"But I agree...maybe at some point in the future. I'm not sure I want to compete with a baby for your attention anytime soon." He carried her into the adjoining bedroom. "You're not getting away from me this time." Then softer, so that she barely heard, he said, "I love you."

Her heart nearly bursting, she wrapped her arms around his neck. "Me too. I love you. But don't you dare think this gives you the leverage to take away my dancing."

"Okay." He drawled out the word as if formulating his argument, but only added, "That's only once in a while." He laid her on the bed.

"Once a week," she added.

He blew out a frustrating sigh. "We'll have to talk about that."

"You have a job that you apparently can't give up. You won't even miss me when I go there for dancing. I'll do it while you're working."

A tic started in his cheek. "I can't protect you there."

She grinned. He cared about her and what she did. A lot. And she liked that. Huskily she said, "Maybe we can work something out." She sat up, leaned forward, and kissed her way down his abdomen.

He laughed, and the sound was carefree and wholehearted. "You're going to be trouble, aren't you?"

"Not if you give me everything I want."

"We'll see."

Chapter Twenty-Four

"Where is she?" Matt plucked at his tuxedo tie, hating its constriction. He glanced down the deserted back hallway of the art museum.

"You know those women," Eli said. "They pop here. They pop there. They pop everywhere. Who knows?"

"I hear the Christmas music starting. That's our signal. She promised she'd be here by now." Matt cursed.

"I'm here. Just…" Kat stumbled into the wall. Her sapphire gown's front drew his eyes right to the silver necklace that disappeared between the swell of her perfect breasts. If the neckline traveled a few centimeters south, he could probably see the top of a nipple. Blood surged to his groin. He took a deep settling breath. He didn't have time to press her into a dark corner. But damn, was she trying to kill him?

"I can't see yet. Give me a sec." She held up her free hand.

He pulled her tight to him. With her soft body pressed against his chest, the tension seeped out of him. He hated the separation when she dimension hopped. When he couldn't track her. Even though Samhain had been a month ago, he was a mess every time she left until she returned, and he got visual confirmation of her safety.

He magically resolved her vertigo and whispered into her ear, "That's an amazing dress."

A throaty laugh erupted from her as she turned into him and wound her hands around his neck. "Such a talented man. God, I love you." She kissed him with an intensity that lit him on fire.

He loved the hoarse way she said his name. "Did you win regionals?"

"Of course. You should've seen Riley. His new outfit is neon-green and black spandex. The man owned it."

"But I know you were the show. You realize that when you dance, you mesmerize the audience."

She pushed away from him. "I win because I'm good at what I do."

He pulled her back to kiss away her pout. "I'll bet you were good."

Eli cleared his throat.

Kat rotated out of his arms to enfold Eli in a hug. She kissed his cheek. Matt ground his back teeth. He hated seeing another man touch her.

She said, "I know I've said this before, Eli, but thank you. For risking your life. For everything. I'm just so glad you've got Matt's back."

Eli's face flushed. He met Matt's gaze. "Strictly platonic. Swear to you."

"If it was anything else, I'd have gutted you last month." He meant it. She was his, and he was about to make sure of it.

"Is Matt keeping you busy?" Kat asked Eli.

Eli shrugged. He met Matt's gaze. "I'm worried about Serenity. There's something going on with her. Even if she is out of MI6…you know how she likes to go off and do her own thing. She's acting erratic."

Matt glared irritation at Eli.

"Sorry," Eli mumbled.

Kat bit her lip. Her worried green gaze shot to Matt. "What are you doing about this?"

"It's under control, wildcat. Don't stress it."

She put her hands on her hips. *Uh-oh.* They may have only been living together for a few weeks, but he knew what the fire in her eyes signaled. "Do I need to call Serenity?"

Matt heard the music enter its final verse. "Sweetheart, can you put that on hold for an hour or so? We're about to be up front and center. We've got to do that dance and then I have to make a speech. There are patrons with deep pockets here tonight that should donate to…shit, I can't even remember which benefit this is."

"Pediatric cancer," Eli supplied.

"Thanks." Matt lifted her left hand. Before she could utter refusal he slipped the ring he'd had specially designed for her onto her finger.

She rotated the diamond-and-emerald ring. "What's this? In my book I already staked my claim."

"We have to do this right for the social world. I don't want anyone thinking you're still on the market. Don't you like it?"

He held his breath while she examined the ring for a few long silent seconds. She glanced up with shining eyes. "It's beautiful. Thank you."

He released his pent up breath and pulled her close. "Marry me, Katherine Ramsey."

"I already did." She placed her hand over the magical tattoo on his chest.

"No, I mean do it right. A wedding with no expense spared…the who's who of society…gigantic cake."

"Okay. But no ice sculptures and no chicken dance. And we're not doing it in Rome."

He chuckled and swept the hair away from her sleek neck

and planted a kiss. He whispered to her, "I love you."

"Did she say yes?" Bryce asked.

"You're goddamned right she did," he replied, releasing her enough that she could turn around to smile at her father.

"Language, please. I think Dad's rubbing off on you." She leaned away from him to kiss her Dad on both cheeks, but Matt didn't release her waist.

Matt said, "If we do a wedding, you'll have to tolerate my mother. I'm sure she'll want to plan the whole thing. She's been salivating at the bit to do a wedding for Allison."

"I get along just fine with your mother. Maybe this is a good project for your sister."

He narrowed his gaze on her. "They do like you…maybe a little too much. Did you do any *special* stuff on them? A little coercion?"

She raised her eyebrows. "I'm charming. Of course they loved me."

"You did. You are a very bad girl, you know." He pulled her tight against his front again.

She murmured, "Very bad." And pulled him in for a kiss.

A few seconds later he ended the kiss. "Stop it. We've got to do this dance. And now the whole world will know I've got a never-ending hard-on for my future wife."

She burst out laughing.

He smiled as he led her toward the dance floor.

She glanced back at Bryce, her concern obvious. He squeezed her hand. "He's fine. I don't think the old geezer is ready to die yet. He likes torturing me."

"I think he wants to stick around to meet his grandchild."

He halted two steps away from the wooden parquet flooring. His gut cramped. It was too soon. Couldn't be. "Are you?"

She nodded. "I'm pretty sure. And I'm scared."

Joy exploded in his chest. He enfolded her in his arms.

"I won't let anything happen to him or you. If I can't…if my ability isn't enough, we will move closer to an Ovate shaman."

"What if I wanted a girl?"

"I'm not ready for a girl. Teenagers…nail polish… dating…another member of the secret Pleiades sisterhood. Nope, it's going to be a boy. She needs a big brother to help me kill any boy that comes close to her. Maybe three big brothers."

A swing-era song surrounded them. He swept her into his arms and they became the focus of attention for the two hundred plus guests in attendance. She whispered, "Girl."

"Boy," he shot back.

She giggled. "You know, this is our first official dance as a couple."

"I'd prefer us to be doing a certain frat-party dance."

Her cheeks scorched. "I had half your clothes off before the song was over. That wouldn't go over too well here."

"I wouldn't mind."

"I didn't suck down three Purple Passion drinks tonight. So, unfortunately, Mr. Ryan, you're safe."

"I am sorry about the morning after. Did you really curse me?"

"I don't know. If I did, it wasn't on purpose. I don't remember exactly what I said. Are you still upset about that? Did it really ruin your life?"

"No." He leaned in and captured her lips. "You're the only one I want to feel this way for."

"Forever?"

He pulled her tighter to him and whispered, "Forever."

Acknowledgments

First and foremost, a huge thank you to three amazing editors who helped bring this story to life: Candace Havens, Allison Collins, and Meredith Johnson. And to the entire Entangled team.

There are so many talented people behind the scenes who help to make a book happen.

Thank you to my husband, Luke, because you're the best for always being willing to discuss action sequences. Thank you for keeping things together when I was running from my day job as a vet to my night job as a writer, and those days of endless rewrites.

To Cait Spivey for helping me whip a rough first draft into shape, thank you.

For once I can't say thank you to Misty the dog since she decided to ingest not one, but two socks during the height of editing stress.

And, as always, thank you to the rest of my incredible family—my parents who are always in my corner. My sister for her endless enthusiasm to read a draft or offer advice. To Jerry for all the love and joy you bring to us. And my son who never hesitates to remind me that "Everything is awesome."

About the Author

Zoe Forward is a hopeless romantic who can't decide between paranormal and urban fantasy romance. So she writes both. In addition to being a mom to one rambunctious kindergartener and wife to a conservation ecologist who plans to save all the big cats on the planet, she's a small animal veterinarian caring for all the small furries, although there is the occasional hermit crab.

When she's not typing at her laptop, she's tying on a karate belt for her son or cleaning up the newest pet mess from the menagerie that occupies her house. She's madly in love with her globe-trotting husband of ten years and happiest when he returns to their home base in North Carolina.

Also by Zoe Forward

HIS WITCH TO KEEP

PLAYING THE WITCH'S GAME

THE WAY YOU BITE

NIGHTSHADE'S BITE

Discover more paranormal romance from Entangled...

Bait N' Witch

a Brimstone, Inc novel by Abigail Owen

Greyson Masters is the Syndicate's best hunter. On top of the danger of his job, Greyson is trying to raise his triplet daughters alone, budding new witches who display an alarming combined power no one understands. Too bad he doesn't have a clue how to deal with them. Until Rowan walks in and the chaos settles for the first time in...well, ever. Little does Greyson know that his new nanny is the elusive witch he's been hunting, and she's been hiding right under his nose this whole time...

Arctic Bite

a Forgotten Brotherhood novel by N.J. Walters

Tracking Cassie Dobbs brings shifter-assassin, Alexei Medvedev, to a remote bar in small-town Alaska, where this hot-as-hell Reaper is casually serving drinks, as if she doesn't have a bounty on her head from Death himself. Alexei is dangerously intrigued. Everyone in the Brotherhood knows the first rule: don't fall for your target. They only send assassins after those who deserve to die...or so he's been made to believe. Now that he's met Cassie, though, he's not so sure.

Bewitching the Enemy

a Vieux Carré Witch Sister novel by Dawn Chartier

Contractor Storm Morgeaux has accidentally set off a series of dark spells hidden in her grandmother's portrait. Desperate to get the spells for themselves, a clan of shape-shifting warlocks have kidnapped Storm's sister to get them. Doctor Nathan Davis is distracted by his stunning new contractor—until she sets off his Paladin medallion. Nathan's first responsibility is eliminating the woman who wields new and dangerous magic. But in order to save her sister, Storm must trust the man who's torn between loving her...and killing her.

Made in the USA
Middletown, DE
06 September 2024